I0456761

Also By Larry Darter

China Doll

A Rick Bishop Novel, 5

Larry Darter

Fedora Press

Copyright © 2023 Larry Darter

All rights reserved.

Thank you for buying an authorized edition of this book. No portion of this book may be reproduced in any form without written permission from the publisher or author, except as permitted by U.S. copyright law.

This is a work of fiction. Names, characters, places, and incidents either are the product of author's imagination or are used fictitiously, and any resemblance to actual person's living or dead, businesses, companies, events, or locales is entirely coincidental.

Paperback ISBN-13: 979-8-9859144-8-1

Contents

Chapter One

It was Thursday. I was singing *It's a Lovely Day Today* as I hung my wash to dry on the clothesline stretched across my Hotel Street second-floor walk up office.

"It's a lovely day today. So whatever you've got to do. You've got a lovely day to do it in. That's true."

The song was an old fifties Doris Day tune. But recently, Volkswagen had featured the song on a television commercial and it was stuck in my head. I took a step back to admire my handiwork. Six shirts, three pairs of socks, and four pairs of boxer shorts.

Times were tough with the Biden inflation, and I had seen nothing resembling a client in over two weeks. After we broke up, my previous girlfriend kicked me out of her house and I lost access to laundry facilities. And thanks to Biden's idea of a robust economy, I couldn't afford to send my laundry out. So I was stuck washing my clothes in my office restroom sink and hanging the wash to air dry. Until I got a paying client and a case that lasted at least a week, I couldn't afford an apartment. Until then, my office did double duty as my residence and I was stuck sleeping on the ratty leather sofa against the back wall. As I threw a few more things into the sink to soak, the phone rang.

I dried my hands on a hand towel. "Okay, okay," I said, walking to the desk. I picked up the receiver.

"Honolulu Confidential Investigations, home of the smiling shamus. Sign up for our new contest and win yourself a genuine Jiffy stainless steel toaster oven."

"Ah, lovely. What must I do?"

"Just send in a postcard, telling us in twenty-five words or less why you love Richard Bishop."

"I can do it in four words."

"What are they?"

"You're a sweet man."

"Oh, you win. You win. Where do you want the toaster oven sent, madam?"

"Send it to 888 Kapiolani Boulevard. But I think I have AC current."

"No problem. That's exactly what the Jiffy requires. And we offer models in three different wattages."

"Oh, Rick, you're ridiculous."

"Hello, baby."

While I didn't have an apartment or laundry facilities since my ex-girlfriend had kicked me out, I had a new girlfriend, the gorgeous and wealthy Sally Jayne Fisher, successful Australian surf culture and beach fashion designer, mining heiress, and socialite. She had long blond hair, beautiful big green eyes, and a figure that was even more attractive than her hundred-million-dollar bank account.

"Hi, Rick. What are you doing?"

"Nothing much. Just doing a little laundry."

"Laundry? It's not Tuesday."

"Yes, Sally, you're right. It isn't Tuesday. But there's nothing going on here, so I thought I'd do some laundry. What's up with you?"

"Oh, nothing really. I just thought I'd call to find out if I'm still seeing you tonight."

"Yes, ma'am. Are we staying in?"

"Well, I thought I'd have Cooper fix dinner and we could sit around and watch a movie or something. But if you would rather go out?"

"No, no, baby. I think that sounds lovely. And so does my wallet."

"Ah, you're broke again?"

"No, just a little bent. I hope that the next client I get is wealthy and brings me a case offering a hefty recovery fee."

"Ah, well, don't you worry about it. I'm sure we can find something fun to do here. I'll see you around eight."

"I'll be there, beautiful."

"See you later, handsome."

"Bye."

As I hung up and turned back toward the bathroom, the phone rang again.

"Yes, dear?" I said after picking up the receiver, thinking Sally was already missing me again. While she probably was, the woman on the line wasn't Sally.

Chapter Two

AFTER A CONFUSED PAUSE, the caller spoke. "Is this Honolulu Confidential Investigations?"

"Yes. Yes, it is. How may I direct your call?"

"I wish to speak with Richard Bishop, please."

"How much does he owe you?"

"What? I don't know what you mean. I wish to hire Mr. Bishop if he is available."

"Let me see if he's available. Can you hold the line, please?" I pressed the phone receiver to my chest and counted to three. Since I was dodging a few collection agencies, I had to be cautious with callers. Clearing my throat, I put the phone back to my ear.

"This is Richard Bishop. How can I help you?"

"Yes, Mr. Bishop. I require the services of a private detective. Are you available?"

"That depends. My fee is three-hundred per day plus expenses. If that's satisfactory, what is your name and what do you wish me to do for you?"

"The fee is acceptable, Mr. Bishop. My name is Nikki Kwan. I'm going to die."

"In that case, Ms. Kwan, you've got the wrong shop. There's a funeral home a few blocks from my office on North Kukui Street."

"Please, Mr. Bishop. Do not joke. I am going to be killed, and I do not want to be killed."

"That's understandable. What do you wish me to do?"

"I want you to protect me. I am prepared to pay. My life is valuable."

"Is it worth three hundred a day, plus expenses?"

"It is worth more than that. I will give you a six-hundred-dollar retainer for protecting me. And another three hundred to deliver an envelope to a man for me."

"Deliver an envelope to whom?"

"Joe Wang, my ex-boyfriend. The man who is going to kill me."

"You want me to take an envelope to the man who's going to kill you?"

"Yes. It is of the utmost importance."

"Why not mail it to him? Even with the price of postage going up all the time, the post office would deliver the envelope for much less than I charge."

"No, there is little time. And I need protection. I will explain the matter to you."

"Please do. It might be helpful."

"Joe got out of prison this morning. He has vowed to kill me. I hope that the contents of the envelope will change his mind."

"You mentioned protection. What do you want me to do?"

"Hide me in a safe place. Then deliver the envelope to Joe... quickly."

"And you're willing to pay me up to nine hundred dollars?"

"Yes. Even more if necessary."

"You've hired yourself a protector. Where do I find Joe?"

"Someplace in Chinatown."

"Chinatown is a big place."

"Joe used to live there, and he owned a nightclub there. But he lost the club and his house when he went to prison. His mother, Irene Chow, still lives there, but I don't know the address. If he isn't living with her, she will know where he is."

I scribbled down the names Joe Wang and Irene Chow.

"Where are you now, Ms. Kwan? Are you bringing the envelope to my office?"

"No. I was on the way there but I saw someone following me. I'm calling from the herbal shop downstairs. The nice lady who owns the shop let me use the phone."

That presented a problem. The woman who owned the Chinese herbal shop below my office was my landlady, Mrs. Wong. There was nothing nice about that old battle axe under the best of circumstances. She was certainly not nice when I was past due on my office rent as I was now, and I had been avoiding her for weeks.

"Well, just walk out of the shop and around the corner. I'll meet you in the alley. You can give me the envelope and I'll take you somewhere safe."

"Someone... someone is outside..." Kwan paused. "I must go now, Mr. Bishop."

"Wait. Where can I meet you?"

"I'll call you when I'm sure no one is following."

Quickly, I gave Kwan my cell phone number. "Call me at that number when you're ready to meet, and I'll come to you as soon as I can get there."

Kwan hung up without replying. I figured she was safe enough with Mrs. Wong. I knew no one in Honolulu who was tough enough to take on that old biddy. Wong scared the bejesus out of me. And the rear exit of the shop opened onto the alley in back, so Kwan could go out that way and give the slip to anyone waiting out front. I hoped she would be okay. I needed the nine hundred bucks.

While I waited for Kwan to call, I intended to rinse the clothes soaking in the sink and, after hanging them, to go see my old friend Lieutenant Chang down at Honolulu PD headquarters on South Beretania Street. When I was on the Honolulu cops, David and I had been partners, and now he was the head of the criminal investigation division. We were still good friends.

Just as I hung the last pair of slacks on the clothesline, the door opened. I couldn't believe it. Two customers in one day. But that is the way of the private investigations racket. It was feast or famine. One minute you're washing socks. The next, you have enough money to stake a claim at every popular joint on Waikiki.

"Are you Richard Bishop?" my visitor said.

I didn't like the looks of him. He was an ugly mug, an Asian guy, mid-thirties, with too much gel in his hair, the Gavin Newsom look. He had on a dark suit without a tie over a black undershirt. No, this guy wasn't a customer.

Chapter Three

THE GUY STARED A hole in me without speaking.

"What can I do for you?"

"I asked if you are Richard Bishop. It is impolite to ignore my question."

"Yeah, sort of as impolite as walking into an office without knocking."

"The sign said to come in."

"How long did you wait before someone came along to read it for you?"

"A comic, huh? Now, are you ready to listen, or must I make you bleed?"

"Oh, it's like that, huh? Okay, I'm listening."

"When you get a call from a Nikki Kwan, turn down the job. You understand? Remember Nikki Kwan. You don't want to work for her."

"That's what you came here to tell me?"

"Yeah. Just a little free advice. I think you better take it if you want to stay healthy."

"What if I don't care what you think?"

The guy slipped his right hand inside his jacket. I'd seen the movie before. So, I bum rushed him. Grabbing his wrist, I put my shoulder into his chest and drove him back hard against the closed door. The breath rushed out of him. It made him forget what he'd reached for. But just to be sure, I punched him in the stomach and he moaned.

Grabbing the lapel of his jacket and jerking him upright, I said, "Here's something to go with it." Then I hit him in the jaw with a right cross that felt good all the way from my fist to my shoulder. That put him to sleep, and he slid down the door to the floor. I reached inside his jacket and pulled a semi-automatic out of the shoulder holster beneath his right arm. Then, grabbing the neck of his jacket, I pulled him across the floor to my desk. I got that lousy feeling again that I had gotten myself into something. Something that already smelled like three-day-old fish. After tossing the gun into a desk drawer, I picked up the phone and dialed.

"Criminal Investigation Division, Detective Sergeant Rowden."

"Rowden, let me talk to the lieutenant."

"Is this Bishop?"

"No, it's the Dalai Lama. Now let me talk to the lieutenant."

"Bishop, what are you going to do when your tired jokes run out?"

"Give them away to idiots. Ready to start your collection?"

All I heard was clicking on the line as Rowden transferred the call."

"Lieutenant Chang."

"Hello David, Bishop."

"Oh, wait a minute. Rowden! Rowden!"

In the distance I heard Rowden answer, "Yes, Lieutenant?"

"Bring me a glass of water. Hold it a minute, Rick."

A moment later, I heard Rowden, now closer, say, "Here you go, Lieutenant." Then I heard a plop, plop, followed by a fizzy noise. About a minute later, David came back on the line.

"Okay, Rick. I drank some Alka-Seltzer. I can stand talking to you for a second."

"If you didn't get so excited, you wouldn't have to drink that stuff."

"I never need this stuff until you call. Now, who's dead?"

"Nobody. But there's a guy in my office lying on the floor."

"Then he's dead. He's got to be."

"No, he isn't, David. I just belted him in the jaw when he tried to get rough."

The guy on the floor started to stir and moan.

"Hang on a minute. He's waking up."

I put the phone next to the guy's mouth. "Groan for the nice police lieutenant."

The guy groaned a little.

"Did you hear him, David?"

"Okay. So what if some guy got tired and went to sleep on your floor. What are you calling me for?"

The guy tried to sit up. "Hold it, David. He's getting a little too active." I punched him in the head and he went back to sleep.

"What did you do?"

"Kissed him goodnight."

"What did you do that for?"

"He tried to pull a gun on me. And he looks like someone wanted for something."

"Oh, well, hang on to him. I'll send a car over."

My cell phone rang. When I pulled it out, I saw on the screen that Nikki Kwan was calling.

"Hold the line for a minute, David. I've got another call." I put down the desk phone receiver and answered the cell phone.

"Bishop."

"Yes, Mr. Bishop, this is Nikki Kwan. I think it's safe to meet you now."

"Okay, Ms. Kwan. Where?"

"Fort DeRussy Beach Park on Kalia Road. I'll be standing near the Hawaii Army Museum building."

Kwan gave me her physical description and said she was wearing a green dress and was holding a fan.

"Okay, I'll be there in twenty or thirty minutes."

"Please hurry, Mr. Bishop. I'm afraid."

"I'll be there as soon as I can," I said. Then we disconnected. I picked up the desk phone receiver.

"Okay, David. Send the car over. I'll leave the door unlocked and will fix him so he doesn't get away."

"Wait a minute, Rick. Where the devil are you going?"

"A little while ago, a woman called me and told me her life was in danger. She hired me to protect her. Then a few minutes later, this guy walked in and told me I better not work for her if I wanted to stay healthy. She just called and asked me to meet her, so I have to get going."

"What do you mean, her life is in danger?"

"She claims her ex-boyfriend intends to kill her. But I haven't got the entire story yet. So, I have to pick her up and stash her somewhere safe until I get a handle on what's going on. Then I'm headed to Sally Fisher's place. Pick this boy up. When you find out who he is and who is working for, you can reach me there."

"Oh, all right, Rick. I'll send Sergeant Rowden over right away."

"Thanks, David."

"Now you listen to me, Rick..."

"Hey, David."

"Yes?"

"Bye."

I hung up the phone. Digging inside a bottom desk drawer, I found another length of clothesline. I dragged the unconscious hood off the floor into a chair and tied him up, putting to use the knot tying skills the Navy had taught me.

"There, that will hold you until the nice policeman comes to collect you." The guy was still out, his head lolled to one side and drool dribbling from his open mouth onto his jacket. He didn't reply.

I grabbed my semi-automatic and holster and clipped the holster to my belt. Honolulu had finally entered the twenty-first century, and the police department was issuing concealed carry permits. David had put in a good word for me with the chief, so now I could pack heat without risking a felony charge.

Not willing to risk an encounter with Mrs. Wong, I climbed out a window, leaped onto the fire escape, and climbed down to the alley. When the old crone had no customers in her shop, as was almost always the case, Wong patrolled the sidewalk out front with her fan broom, denying access to the three parking spaces in front of her shop. Those she reserved for her nonexistent customers. I straightened my jacket, left the alley and walked to the corner of North Hotel and Maunakea Street. Five minutes later, I boarded the number 20 bus for Waikiki.

Besides not having an apartment, I also didn't have a car. Some government punks from the mainland had shot up and burned my new Mustang during a previous case. My insurer had refused to pay my claim. My agent said I hadn't notified them I used the car for business and that since I didn't pay for the additional coverage, the company wasn't liable under the policy terms. I disagreed and hired my friend and attorney, Nicole Hersey, to sue and bring the crooked insurance company to its knees by forcing them to pay my claim. But thus far, the insurer hadn't capitulated, leaving me dependent on mass transit, taxicabs, and shoe leather for basic transportation.

About twenty minutes later, I stepped off the bus at the corner of Kalia Road and Saratoga. Then I walked two blocks to the beach park. When I arrived, I saw an Asian girl wearing a short green dress and holding a Chinese hand fan loitering beneath a palm tree near the side of the museum building. When I say girl, I mean she was gorgeous. She was gorgeous in the way a girl would have looked to the Tom Hanks' character in Castaway after the plane crash had stranded him on a desert island for four years with only a soccer ball named Wilson for company. I still shuddered to think of the things Hanks must have done to that poor soccer ball. Anyway, the scandalously short and tight dress hugged her voluptuous body like shrink-wrap on a rump roast. I walked over, struggling to catch my breath.

"Ms. Kwan?"

Kwan lowered the big sunglasses she wore and peered at me over the rims. Her big brown eyes looked like pools of melted chocolate I could imagine happily drowning in. I fought the desperate urge to grab her fan to cool myself down.

"Mr. Bishop?"

"Yes, but please, call me Rick. All my friends do and I have a feeling we'll become fabulous friends."

"Very well, Rick," Kwan said shyly. "You may call me Nikki."

Having spent most of my life in the melting pot of Hawaii, I recognized Nikki Kwan was of Chinese extraction. But instead of Chinese accented English, her accent sounded British. I assumed that meant she hailed originally from Hong Kong.

"Have you someplace safe in mind for me to stay until you have delivered the envelope?" she asked.

"Not yet. But I have loads of friends all over Oahu. I'm sure I know someone who will take you in. Let's walk up the street to a nearby coffee shop. You can tell me the full story over coffee and then I'll arrange someplace safe for you to stay."

Kwan nodded in agreement and we strolled arm in arm up Kalia to the nearby coffee purveyor at the Hilton Hawaiian Village. There Kwan ordered a cold brew, and I got black coffee. Then we sat at a table near the back that afforded us adequate privacy, and Nikki shared her tale of woe.

Chapter Four

KWAN STARED DOWN AT the table after finishing her story, unwilling to meet my gaze. "So, you see, Joe and I were lovers. I suppose I've always had a taste for the bad boy type. Right after they sent him to prison five years ago, I went to visit him. Joe told me he knew I had tipped off the police and got him arrested. That is when he said he would kill me as soon as he got out of jail."

I had trouble imagining the beautiful, soft-spoken woman across the table as a moll, the companion of a mobster like Joe Wang. I'd never dealt with Wang when I was on the cops, but vaguely knew him by reputation. Kwan seemed so pure and innocent. Of course, Congressman Eric Swalwell had probably thought the same about Christine Fang, the communist Chinese spy he had reportedly slept with for a while after she snagged him in her honey trap.

"Did you drop the dime on him?"

"No. But I know who did. I kept asking around Chinatown discreetly until I learned who had tipped the police to Joe's gambling business. Then, I got close to the man until I got the chance to record a conversation with my phone, where the man bragged to an associate about taking Joe down."

"Who are we talking about?"

"His name is Jimmy Cho, Joe's longtime rival in Chinatown. After the authorities seized Joe's home and nightclub through civil asset forfeiture, claiming Joe used the property to commit criminal activities, Cho bought the nightclub at auction and reopened it."

"What club did Joe own?"

"China Doll."

"Ah, yes, the China Doll."

China Doll was everything you would expect in a Chinatown nightclub. It was a hostess bar; strip club, and a place where local gangsters hung out. The club featured exotic dancers and was a favorite among the sailors and marines stationed around Honolulu and the local motorcycle clubs such as the Devil's Spawn. Since the early sixties, owners of the China Doll operated what appeared a legitimate nightclub on the first floor. They operated a bar, served upscale food and drinks, and hosted live music and dancing. But upstairs was a different story. The second floor, called the Playroom, was where the real action took place—the hostesses who also worked as prostitutes, the strippers, cocaine sales, and gambling.

Nikki told me she had gone to work for Joe Wang as the headliner singer at the first-floor nightclub after moving to Honolulu from Hong Kong. They eventually struck up a relationship and became lovers.

"So, tell me, Nikki, what's inside the envelope you want me to deliver to Joe?"

"A flash drive containing the recording I mentioned. I hope when Joe hears the recording, he will understand Jimmy Cho tipped the police and change his mind about killing me."

"That might work if I can find him."

Kwan removed a manila, legal-size envelope from her handbag, along with another envelope containing a thick stack of twenties. She slid them across the table. She had sealed the envelope containing the flash drive, but I felt it through the paper. I opened the other and glanced at the twenties.

"The six-hundred-dollar retainer I promised is in the second envelope. I have another three hundred ready to pay you as soon as you deliver the sealed envelope to Joe."

"Leave it with me," I said, slipping the two envelopes into my inside jacket pocket. "You're in good hands."

"But the matter of a safe place for me to wait until you make the delivery remains."

"Don't worry, sweetheart. I have someone in mind I'm sure will help. She's a good friend who owes me a favor and is also my attorney. She has an office near the Honolulu District Court on Alakea Street. We'll grab a cab and I'll take you down and introduce you."

Kwan smiled for the first time since we'd met and seemed to relax. "May I ask you a question, Rick?"

"Certainly."

"You are quite handsome. Tell me, Rick. Are you the bad boy type?"

"Well, I can be," I grinned. "But only in the nicest ways, if you catch my drift."

Kwan beamed. "Perhaps after you resolve this horrible matter, we might have dinner and get better acquainted."

"Oh, my. That sounds like a lovely idea."

Of course, I'd need an excuse to break a date with a certain Australian blonde I kept company with every evening to swing a night out with Nikki. But I was resourceful in that department. I had more excuses than a pregnant nun when a situation like Nikki Kwan presented itself.

"Come along, honey," I said, standing up. "We have a cab to catch and miles to go before we sleep."

As we strolled out of the coffee shop, I slipped an arm around her waist, just to make her feel safe. I knew how women appreciated a sense of security. And when my palm slipped south for a light caress of her magnificent backside, Nikki didn't seem to mind. Instead, she basked in the warm glow of safety she felt in the company of a rough, six-two, muscular private investigator who stood ready to do violence on those who would harm her.

Out in front of the hotel, I had a porter hail us a taxi. With six hundred dollars in my pocket, I splurged for a taxi instead of asking Nikki to take the bus. Now, if only I could persuade the other Nikki in my life, Nicole Hersey, to take in my client as a short-term house guest, I could soon get busy finding Joe Wang and collect my three-hundred-dollar bonus.

Chapter Five

AFTER GETTING IN THE taxi, Nikki and I were soon holding hands. But I could tell from her sweaty palm and pinched expression she felt nervous again. She kept glancing back over her shoulder as if expecting pursuers.

"Relax, dear," I said, letting go of her hand so I could caress her stocking covered thigh. "You're safe with me."

"I'm frightened the man I saw outside your office might have tracked us down by now."

"No need to worry your pretty little head about him," I said. "I'm sure I left that man tied to a chair in my office before I came to meet you."

"What?"

"Yes, right after you called, a man in a black suit with excessive hair gel called at my office. He told me to turn down your case when you called me. So, I roughed him up a little, tied him to a chair, and called a friend at HPD to come collect him. I'm sure he is in jail by now."

"Yes, that sounds like the man I saw," Nikki said, relaxing and laying her head on my shoulder.

"That reminds me, sweetheart. Who else knew you planned to talk to me? Someone must have told that guy you intended to come to me for help."

"Only my closest friend knew and she wouldn't betray me."

"Who is she?"

"Lucy Wong. We used to work together at China Doll. I told her I needed someone to deliver the envelope to Joe and suggested hiring a private detective. Lucy and I used her computer to search and found your website."

I sure hoped that Lucy Wong was no relative of my landlady. Mrs. Wong would sell out her best friend in a heartbeat just to move a few bottles of licorice root.

"Is Lucy a professional singer like you?"

"No, Lucy was an exotic dancer at the club. But she is a good person."

"I have nothing against strippers. I have more respect for girls who get naked for tips than those unemployed women with doctorates in gender studies living on welfare and trying to persuade Uncle Joe into dumping their student loan debt on to the backs of hard-working lunch bucket taxpayers like me. Stripping is good, honest work. Does she still work at China Doll?"

"No, we all lost our jobs when the police arrested Joe. They shut the club down. We shared an apartment, but I couldn't stay there with Joe getting out of prison. He knew where I lived. Lucy couldn't afford the rent alone. So, we both moved out a week before Joe got out of jail."

"Where does Lucy live now?"

"I don't know. I've tried calling and texting, but Lucy hasn't responded since the day after we moved out of the apartment."

"Hmm, that seems odd."

"I just hope Joe hasn't done something to Lucy," Nikki said, the big tears that had welled in her pretty brown eyes spilling down her beautiful cheeks.

"There, there, honey," I said, pulling out my handkerchief and wiping her tears. "You'll ruin your mascara."

As I put the handkerchief away, I noticed I had gotten a little of her bright red lipstick on it accidentally.

Finally, the taxi pulled up in front of Nicole's office building. I paid the driver, and we entered the building and took the elevator up to Nicole's floor. Her secretary, a cute little redhead named Mandy, told me Nicole was in court but should be back within the hour. Mandy sported a Dutch boy hair cut that looked darling on her. She was a little on the waifish side, but I figured she could have me barking at the moon with little effort. Sadly, Mandy didn't like me much because she thought I used her boss and didn't give back much in return. Who needed the hostility? So, bidding Mandy farewell, I took Nikki back downstairs and out of the building. We walked over to the Honolulu District Court on Alakea Street at the intersection with Hotel Street and waited beside the front steps for Nicole.

"Rick, can't I stay at your place until you deliver the envelope instead of staying with your attorney friend? I'd sleep so much better with you nearby at night."

Nikki probably wouldn't enjoy sharing the ratty couch in my office, so I sadly shook my head. "No, baby. My place is a little cramped and you will find Nicole's place much more comfortable."

"Then, can you stay there with me, just for a few nights, until you find Joe and give him the envelope?"

"No. See, Nicole and I have a little romantic history and even if she agreed I could stay, it would be awkward for everyone."

Indeed, Nicole and I had had a brief fling during a previous case, the same one where the rogue government agents torched my Mustang. That fling caused the breakup with my girlfriend at the time, Gabby Inouye. Oddly, I'd even proposed marriage to Nicole, and she had accepted. But luckily, she changed her mind, and the romance withered and died a natural death.

Nicole came out the front doors of the courthouse wearing a sharp tan business suit jacket over a navy blouse with a matching tan skirt that hit well above her knees and navy pumps with four-inch heels. She looked surprised to see me standing at the foot of the stairs with a gorgeous woman clinging to me. Or maybe she looked more aghast than surprised.

"Rick, what are you doing here?" she snapped.

"Hi, Nicole. How's my best girl?"

Nicole rolled her eyes, glared at Nikki, and then wheeled and walked away down the sidewalk. Nikki and I hurried to catch up and fell into step beside her. Finally, Nicole stopped, turned, and glared at me.

"What?"

"I need a small favor."

"A favor!" Nicole's open mouth formed a perfect "O" after she had uttered the final syllable. Her nostrils flared, and her wide-eyes bulged until I feared they might escape her head. "What makes you think I'd do you a favor, you jerk?"

"Because we're close friends, and I'm always willing to do favors for you."

"Since when? You're already screwing me over the lawsuit you asked me to file as a favor. You owe me five thousand in legal fees so far and you haven't paid a penny."

"You know I'm good for it, Nicole. As soon as you win the suit and collect from the insurance company, I'll pay you every dollar owed."

"Rick, I didn't take your case on a contingency basis. You agreed to pay me. And if the case goes to court, it is far from a sure thing you will win. You didn't take out the business rider on that policy to save a few bucks, and the insurance company may not have to pay out on the claim."

"Nevertheless, I'm good for it. And I never refuse when you ask me for a favor."

"When have you ever done me a favor, Rick, my boy? Name one."

"Well, I proposed that time."

"Ha. You call that a favor? Proposing? Your psychopathic girlfriend almost killed me and you over that favor."

"Don't worry. Gabby isn't my girlfriend anymore. I have a new one."

"So I see," Nicole said, cutting her eyes toward Nikki.

"Oh, this isn't my girlfriend. She's a client. Let me introduce you."

Turning to Nikki, who had recoiled in horror at Nicole's angry outburst, I took her by the elbow and pulled her closer.

"Nikki Kwan, meet my dearest friend, Nicole Hersey, the finest legal mind in Hawaii. Nicole, this is Nikki."

Nicole rolled her eyes again.

"It's a pleasure to meet you, Ms. Hersey," Nikki said, tentatively extending her hand.

"Charmed, I'm sure," Nicole said, ignoring Nikki's outstretched hand. Turning to me, she said with sarcasm, "Well, what a coincidence. You've found another Nikki."

"Well, yes, but it is only coincidental. Nikki just hired me today. Besides, you never liked it when I called you Nikki. You've always insisted on Nicole."

Nicole looked at her watch. "Let's wrap this up, Richard. I need to get back to the office."

"Well, someone is targeting Nikki here for death," I said. "I need a safe place for her to stay. Just for a few days until I can resolve her problem."

Nicole dropped her head and snorted like a bull ready to charge. Then she glared at me, reached out, and grabbed a fistful of my jacket lapels.

"Please excuse us for a moment, Ms. Kwan," she said, before dragging me several feet away.

"Hey," I said, prying her fingers from my jacket. I just had this suit cleaned and you're wrinkling the lapels.

"You have some nerve, Richard Bishop. No, I am not taking one of your skanks into my home. Nope. Not happening. And I don't want to see you again unless you have a check for five thousand dollars in your grubby little paw."

"Please, Nicole. It isn't like that. Nikki is only a client. I'm desperate and have no one else I trust as much as you to turn to. Just two nights. I beg of you. Three tops. Her life is in grave danger. Do you want her death on your conscience?"

"Only a client? Please. I saw the way she was hanging all over you and looking at you with those big puppy dog eyes. If you aren't sleeping with her, you soon will be. Keep her at your place."

"I can't. Honestly, I'm going through a rough patch right now and bunking on the couch at my office. I don't even have a shower there."

"Gross. You aren't showering? I thought I smelled something funky."

"I shower every other day at my gym," I said defensively, lifting my right arm and sniffing at my armpit.

"I'm not taking her into my home, Richard. Get that through your thick Neanderthal skull."

"But I have no one else to turn to."

"You said you have a new girlfriend. Let her take in the tart."

"Come on, Nicole. You know how awkward that would be. Like you, Sally would jump to the wrong conclusions. And I don't know Sally well enough yet to ask her to take in a stranger."

"No. Rick. No."

Once she started calling me Rick again instead of Richard, I knew Nicole was weakening. I played my hole card to close the deal.

"This is a big case that will net me thousands in fees. I'd be able to pay you something toward the legal fees in return for one tiny favor."

I watched Nicole's expression, almost able to see the squirrel cage turning slowly inside her head.

"How much will you pay me? The five thousand you owe me to date?"

"Be reasonable, Nicole. I can't afford to pay it all in one chunk. But I'll make a serious dent in the five thousand owed as soon as I collect my fee."

"How much cash do you have on you right now?"

"I only collected a small retainer. I can't pay you until Nikki pays me the big bonus after I finish the job."

"How much is the bonus?"

"Twenty-five hundred," I lied. I hated lying to Nicole, but desperate circumstances require desperate measures.

"All right, Rick. You swear to hand over the twenty-five hundred and I'll do it. And we'll work out a repayment plan for the balance. But it's two nights only. If you haven't resolved things after two nights, you will promptly pick up Miss Hottie or I'll put her out on the curb."

"Oh, all right. If it's the only way to keep Nikki alive, I'll bow to your cruel demands."

Nicole beamed, making former quarterback Johnny Manziel's finger rubbing "money" gesture with both hands. "Don't even think about screwing me on this deal, Rick. If you do, I'll make sure you regret it."

"Okay, okay. You'll get your blood money, and I promise only two nights."

"Fine. I should be home by six this evening. You can drop her off after six."

"I need you to take Nikki now," I said. "With only two days to work with, I have to get busy derailing the plan to kill her. Just take her back to the office with you. She's a super nice girl and very bright. I'm sure she will be happy to help with running copies or something."

"I can't babysit her at work and I won't take off early just to take her home now, Rick."

"She won't be any trouble and we will both be so grateful, Nicole. I'm sure she will be very helpful. Just turn her over to Mandy."

Nicole glanced at her watch again. "Okay fine. I'm exhausted from arguing with you, Rick. I should have been back at the office ten minutes ago."

"Thank you, thank you, Nicole," I said, grabbing her in a bear hug. "I owe you one."

"Unhand me," she said, pushing me away. "And take a shower, will you? You smell."

Chastened, I hurried back to Nikki, took her elbow, and guided her to Nicole.

"Nicole is happy to have you as a houseguest for a few nights, Nikki."

"Two nights," Nicole corrected.

"Thank you, Ms. Hersey. I'm very grateful for your kindness."

Nicole nodded. "Well, come on, toots. You're going back to the office with me until I finish work so that Sam Spade here can solve all your problems."

"Thank you, Rick," Nikki said, enveloping me in a hug and kissing my cheek.

"That's what I do, sweetheart," I said, squeezing her bottom with both hands. "Trouble is my business."

Nicole yanked Nikki out of my grasp, flipped me the finger, and then, taking Nikki by the arm, led her away down the sidewalk toward the law office building.

I stood and enjoyed the view until the women melted into the crowd. Nikki had a marvelous derriere and walked with a sway I found hypnotic. But Nicole's rear end, in or out of a tight-fitting skirt, was magnificent too, as I well-remembered from our brief engagement.

With Nikki taken care of, I saw no need to waste precious funds on a taxi. So, I trudged to the stop on Alakea Street and waited for the bus. When the bus arrived, I climbed aboard, thinking I had reduced my problems by half after securing a safe house for Nikki. All I had to do now was find Joe Wang and deliver the envelope. Little did I know my problems were only beginning.

Chapter Six

IT WAS HOT AND stuffy on the bus. I wanted to take off my jacket but couldn't because of the gun on my hip. After I collected from Nikki, maybe I'd invest in a snub-nosed revolver and an ankle holster for summer wear. My phone rang and when I pulled it out, I saw the call was from Honolulu PD. I didn't feel like a conversation with David, so I pressed ignore. Right away, the phone rang again. I switched it to silent and put it back into my pocket. David would have to wait. Right now, I felt tired and in desperate need of a little tender loving care. I knew just where I could get my belly rubbed and other things that would make me feel better, at the home of a beautiful blonde named Sally Jayne Fisher.

About ninety minutes after boarding the bus on Alakea and many transfers later, I got off the bus and walked the last three blocks from the bus stop to the Fisher abode at 888 Kapiolani Boulevard. Sally owned a luxury spacious top floor, four bedroom, four bath condominium with stunning mountain and Koko Head views during the day from the dramatic ten-foot floor-to-ceiling windows in every room. In the evenings, the views of the glittering Honolulu city lights were just as magnificent. I took the elevator to the fourth floor and rang the doorbell. Cooper, her houseboy, opened the door.

"Good evening, Mr. Bishop."

"Good evening, Cooper. Is Ms. Fisher in?"

"Yes, sir," Cooper said, standing aside to allow me to enter. "She's in the lounge, sir," he said, closing the door. The lounge, I had long since learned, was what Australians called the living room.

"A beer would be nice."

"Yes, sir. Mr. Bishop, if you don't mind me saying so, I really love the way you talk."

"Well, thank you, Cooper. I suppose hearing an Australian accent all the time must get tiring."

"Oh, Mr. Bishop," Cooper chuckled. "You're pulling my leg again."

Cooper left for the kitchen and I repaired to the lounge. With Nikki Kwan out of sight, if not out of mind, I could again concentrate on enjoying the company of the woman I loved.

"Anyone home?"

"Rick, you're early. It's just half-past five. Hi."

"Hi."

Sally wore an outfit that looked like silk pajamas. As a trained observer, I noted she wore no bra beneath the top. A brief glimpse of heaven. I felt my vigor returning. I took off my jacket, tossed it on a chair, and then loosened my tie before dropping onto the couch beside her. Sally tucked her legs beneath her and snuggled up against me and I took her in my arms and kissed her.

"Is that a gun I feel or are you just happy to see me?" Sally said with a giggle.

"Oh, sorry, I forgot," I said, leaning away and unclipping the holster from my belt. I put the holstered pistol on the end table and resumed where we had left off.

"How was your day, darling?"

"Tiring."

"Oh, poor baby. All that laundry?"

"Well, doing laundry is tiring enough, but I also got a client and then had to beat up a guy that tried to get rough with me in the office."

"What?" Sally said, sitting upright. "You got a client?"

"Yes, I did."

"A man or a woman?"

"Woman."

"Is she attractive?"

"Oh, maybe a little. Nothing like you, baby."

"Blonde or brunette?"

"Both."

"Both? A blonde with dark roots?"

"No, a brunette with a blonde disposition."

"I see."

"New outfit?"

"Yes. Do you like it? It's called lounge wear."

"Huh? I've been inside many lounges, but I've never seen an outfit like that. And yes, I love it. But do you think it wise to go braless in front of the hired help?"

"Oh, Rick, you're so awful," Sally laughed. "You know Cooper is gay, right?"

"Really? That explains something. I think he just made a pass at me when I came in."

"What? A pass?"

"Yes, he told me he really loved the way I talk. Now that I think about it, he looked a little wistful when he said it."

Sally laughed out loud. "Rick, you idiot. I'm sure he only meant your American accent differs from ours."

"So, you think it was an innocent remark instead of a pass."

"Well, I don't know. You do have a *purty* mouth."

We both laughed at that one. "Did you watch *Deliverance* this afternoon?"

Sally grinned. "No, but I've seen it before." She leaned over and kissed me. Then she sat bolt upright and snatched the handkerchief from my pocket.

"What's this?" she said, pointing a long manicured, polished nail at the lipstick on the handkerchief. "Is this hers?"

"My client's lipstick? Yes. That shade doesn't go well with my complexion. I never use it."

"Wait," she said, inspecting my shirt collar. "There's more of it on your collar. Just what kind of work are you doing for this client?"

"Oh, honey, it's nothing to worry about. She cried, and I lent her my handkerchief. She must have gotten a little lipstick on it?"

"Then she dried her tears on your shirt collar?"

"No, she was only showing her gratitude to me for saving her life. Her lips must have brushed my collar when she gave me a sisterly hug."

"Sisterly, huh?" Sally said before crossing her arms and sticking out her bottom lip.

"Oh, come on, baby. You're the only woman for me. You know that."

"Don't talk to me. I'm mad."

"Oh, honey, don't be mad. I've been looking forward to seeing you all day long."

"Really?"

"Yes, it's all I've thought about. I could barely concentrate on work."

"Well, I might forgive you. In time."

Cooper returned from the kitchen and handed me a glass and a cold bottle of Longboard lager. "Dinner will be ready in half an hour, Ms. Fisher. I hadn't expected Mr. Bishop until eight."

"That's fine, Cooper. Mr. Bishop is rather busy at the moment convincing me why I shouldn't throw him out."

"Oh, dear," Cooper said with raised eyebrows. "Good luck, sir," he said, retreating to the kitchen.

"Where did you find old Cooper, anyway? He's a little old for a houseboy."

"Cooper isn't that old. Anyway, Father gave him to me as a housewarming present when he bought me the condo. Cooper worked for us in Sydney. Father knows I'm rubbish with domestic skills."

"That's okay, baby. You have other marvelous skills I've learned to appreciate. I could truly benefit from those skills this evening after such a tiring day."

Sally laughed. "You appreciate my skills, do you? Could have fooled me, since it seems you've been playing kissy face with your female client all day."

"Oh, honey. I've done no such thing. Let's forget about her and focus on you. You want me to teach you how to play post office?"

"Oh, Rick, you're awful," Sally chuckled. "And the answer is no. I'm still mad."

"I'm mad too, darling. Mad about you. Come here and give us a kiss. I've had such a tiring day."

"Aw, poor baby. You want mummy to make it all better?"

"Yes, please. I'm starved for affection."

The phone rang.

"Pardon me," Cooper said, reentering the room and picking up the phone.

"Ms. Fisher's residence."

"Yes, sir. One moment, sir."

"It's for you, Mr. Bishop," Cooper said, offering me the phone. "It's a Lieutenant Chang, sir, with the Honolulu Police."

"Thank you, Cooper," I said, taking the phone.

"Yes, David? What is it?"

"Rick, you get right down here."

"What?"

"Get down here to the station, Bishop. You're in trouble. The guy you called about this morning was dead when Sergeant Rowden arrived."

"Now, wait a minute, David. Dead? He was fine when I left him."

"Not dead, huh? Just when my stomach is getting back to normal, you knock some guy off."

"Knock some guy off?"

"I don't know why I wasted time calling you. I should have sent Rowden out to get you and had him drag you here in handcuffs. But I didn't because I like your girlfriend too much to do that to her."

"What are you babbling about?"

"I thought you said the guy in your office was still kicking when you called."

"He was."

"Oh, yeah? Well, somebody filled his chest full of bullet holes. And I like you for a suspect. Now, get down here."

"Wait a minute, David. Someone shot him to death?"

"Yeah. Either that or he died of fright when he saw the bullets coming toward him. Now, I'm not talking anymore until you get here. Get here in thirty minutes, or I'll put a warrant out for you."

Before I could reply, David slammed the phone down.

"Oh, swell," I said, hanging up the phone.

"Rick, what's the matter?" Sally asked.

"Oh, that crazy David Chang is trying to hang a murder rap on me."

"Murder?" Sally said, her hand flying to her mouth. "Oh, Rick, who did you kill?"

"I didn't kill anyone, Sally. David has his wires crossed. But I have to go down to the station and get it cleared up."

"Who does David think you killed?"

"That guy I told you about. He came to my office and threatened me. He said I shouldn't take the case I took this morning. When he reached for a gun, I smacked him and knocked him out. Then I tied him to a chair and called David to come pick him up."

"Did you hit him too hard?"

"No, honey. He was alive and breathing when I left the office. Someone shot him. I left the door unlocked for the police when I left to meet my client. By the time Rowden got there, probably after stopping off for a bag of donuts, someone must have walked into my office and shot him."

"I'll have Cooper postpone dinner and I'll drive you to the police station."

"No honey. I'll get a cab. I don't know how long this is going to take."

"All right, darling, but you will come back later, won't you? Cooper can save you some dinner."

"I can't promise," I said glumly. "Now, on top of everything else, I might have to go looking for the killer to clear myself."

"Oh, Rick. I wanted us to spend time together tonight."

"I'm sorry, baby. If I don't make it back tonight, I'll see you tomorrow evening."

"Rick, if we..."

I turned away because the taxi service had answered the phone. They said a cab had just dropped off a fare in the neighborhood and could pick me up in less than five minutes. I told the dispatcher I'd be waiting outside and hung up.

"I've got to run, sweetheart." I said, clipping my holster to my belt and shrugging into my jacket. "Love you."

"But, Rick."

I kissed her and then walked out of the room, just barely hearing her parting words.

"If we got married, things like this wouldn't happen."

I cringed. Talk of marriage always gave me panic attacks.

Chapter Seven

I WALKED INTO DAVID Chang's office in a foul mood. He started in on me as soon as I sat down.

"Now look, Rick. I don't care what you say. You told me you had a guy in your office. When Sergeant Rowden got there, he found him tied to a chair with three bullet holes in his chest."

"David, he was making noises when I left."

"Guys often do that when someone shoots them."

"Oh, stop being an idiot." I pulled my semi-automatic, dumped the magazine, and put it down on his desk. "Check it. I have not fired it lately. Then maybe you'll believe I didn't kill him."

"I know you didn't kill him with that."

David opened his desk drawer, took out a plastic evidence bag, and slammed it on the desk. Inside I saw the bag contained the gun I had taken off the guy that morning and left in my desk drawer.

"That's the murder weapon?"

"We haven't sent it to ballistics yet, but that's the way it looks. Maybe you can explain how your fingerprints got on that gun. I need something to tell the chief."

"I told you on the phone the guy pulled a gun on me. That's the explanation. I took it off him after I knocked him cold and left it in my desk drawer. If you've already found my prints on it, then you found these."

I held up my right thumb and forefinger.

"I didn't even grip it. I only used two fingers to pull it out of his holster. And I guarantee you didn't get my print off the trigger because I never touched it. Whoever shot the guy used gloves and left my prints on it. But the positioning will be all wrong and will prove I didn't fire that gun."

"Okay, Rick. I've known you a long time. I know you didn't kill him. But am I supposed to let you off because we're friends and you used to be on the force without bringing you in for questioning when your prints are on the murder gun?"

"No, but you don't have to act like I shot up half of Chinatown."

"Well, I'm mad. I want to retire in a few years. And I want to do it with a healthy stomach."

"Now you know why my prints were on the gun. And you called me here before I washed up for dinner. I haven't washed my hands since I got up this morning. So, test my hands for gunshot residue. I insist on it."

David's phone rang.

"Yeah, what is it, Rowden?"

"I got the information on the dead guy's prints, Lieutenant."

"Then bring it in, Rowden. And bring a GSR test with you."

"Yes, Lieutenant."

David and I scowled at each other until Rowden came in. I held up my hands.

"You want me to test the gumshoe for GSR, Lieutenant?"

"I didn't call you in here to test me, Rowden. I didn't shoot the guy. Now, give me those papers."

"Yes, Lieutenant."

David flipped through the documents Rowden brought while the sergeant swabbed my hands for gunshot residue. It was a presumptive test and a few minutes later, Rowden announced the test was negative.

"Thanks, Rowden. That will be all. Get out of here."

"Yes, Lieutenant."

Rowden walked out of the office, closing the door behind him. I wiped my hands with my handkerchief.

"Care to share, David?"

"Yeah, the guy's name is Chong Pong. I've heard of him. He's a shooter with a rap sheet a mile long. Let's see. Yeah, he's done two prison stretches. One for aggravated assault with a deadly weapon and one for manslaughter."

"Any connection with a guy named Joe Wang?"

"Joe Wang? Why do you ask?"

"My client claims Joe Wang, her ex-boyfriend, threatened to kill her."

"Last I heard, Joe Wang is in prison doing a nickel on a gambling promotion conviction. The county took his nightclub and house with civil asset forfeiture."

"They did, but Wang finished his sentence. He's out now."

"I hadn't heard. Anyway, to answer your question, Chong Pong was an independent. He worked for any mobster willing to pay him. So, there is no connection with Wang as far as I know."

"It doesn't stack anyway."

"What doesn't stack?"

"That Joe Wang would have sent Chong Pong to scare me off my case or had someone kill him. My client only wants me to deliver something to Wang that proves she didn't drop the dime on him that got him arrested and convicted. He thinks she did, and that's why he threatened to kill her when he got out of prison. But she got the proof someone else tipped the cops."

"What kind of proof?"

"She recorded someone bragging about taking Wang down and getting him sent to prison."

"Did she tell you who?"

"Jimmy Cho."

"Ah, right. Another Chinatown gangster. He took over the China Doll nightclub after Joe Wang went to prison. And I'm sure he's running all the same rackets."

"What was the gambling rap they sent Wang up the river on? The gambling on the second floor of the club?"

"No. No one ever paid that any attention, and everyone in Honolulu knew about it. Joe Wang got greedy. He bought a 232-foot, 1,500 passenger ship. He advertised it as a dinner cruise and whale watching excursion for tourists as a cover. The ship sailed from Pier 6 at Aloha Tower seven nights a week for eight-hour cruises and Wang operated a full-scale casino onboard. About five years ago, someone tipped off the vice boys, and they got a search warrant. One night when the ship docked, they raided it, arrested the operators, including Wang, and seized the ship. They tied it to Wang's other criminal enterprises and wiped him out."

"No wonder he wants the person dead who dropped the dime."

"But it was Jimmy Cho, not your client?"

"Right. She says the recording proves it and she hopes when I deliver it to Wang, he will change his mind about killing her."

"Think it will work?"

I shrugged. "I haven't heard the recording. She sealed it in an envelope I'm supposed to deliver to Wang. I'm only telling you what she told me. She seems to think it might get her out of Wang's crosshairs."

"Well, it's still screwy. If Wang is after blood, you can bet there will be a murder. If not your client, then Cho. And my guess is, whether or not it stacks, the murder of Chong Pong connects to it."

"Maybe Cho sent him to frighten me away from helping my client. Maybe he found out about the recording. But I can't figure any motive Cho had to kill Chong Pong. Maybe Wang is behind it. Maybe he heard rumors about the recording already and wants me to bring the recording to him."

"Could be. One way to find out. Deliver the recording to Joe Wang."

"I intend to as soon as I can find him. My client doesn't know where he is living after he got out of prison."

"I don't know either. I didn't even know he got out. But I know someone who could probably tell you where to find him."

"Who?"

"An old bird named Glenda Mills."

"Glenda Mills," I said, stroking my chin. "I haven't seen Glenda since I arrested her for robbery when I was still a cop. She used to get sailors and marines to buy her drinks in bars and let them think they were going to get lucky. She spiked their drinks before they went up to her hotel room, where they promptly passed out. Then she rolled them and left them in the room."

"Yeah, that's Glenda. But she is just an old alcoholic now. She doesn't have the looks for the racket anymore and claims she has gone straight."

"Well, I never remember Glenda being all that attractive."

"She was attractive enough for drunk sailors back in the day. But now her face looks like she had an argument with a nail gun and lost it. No one could get drunk enough without dying of alcohol poisoning to find Glenda attractive now. But you can bet she still knows about everything criminal going on in Chinatown. If you can get her to talk, I'll bet she can tell you where to find Joe Wang."

"Where do I find Glenda?"

"You can find her any day you like at the Harbor Lounge on Kalani Street."

I looked at my watch and saw it wasn't even nine.

"Well, if we're done here, I think I'll head to the Harbor Lounge. It's still early for the professional drinkers."

"You want me to send Rowden along?"

"No, I want to ask Glenda questions, not give her a heart attack."

"Rick, lay off Rowden. He isn't that bad."

"I don't dislike Rowden. He just reminds me too much of Lurch from that old *Addams Family* television show. An uglier version of Lurch."

"Oh, knock of it off, Rick. Leave Rowden alone."

David picked up the phone. "Rowden, I'm turning Bishop loose. Go down the street to the drugstore and get me a box of Alka-Seltzer. The large box. Then bring it to me with a glass of water. And, Rowden, shut up. Don't you dare say, 'Yes, Lieutenant.' Now get going."

David slammed the phone down. I picked up my pistol, inserted the magazine, and stuck the gun back into my holster.

"Listen to me, Rick. Don't you dare shoot anyone tonight. I've already got one stiff thanks to you and I don't want anymore. And one more thing..."

"Hey, David?"

"What?"

"Bye."

I walked out of the office and headed for the elevator.

Chapter Eight

DAVID HAD BEEN RIGHT on both counts. I found Glenda sitting at the bar when I walked into the Harbor Lounge. And David hadn't exaggerated when he said she was ugly. She reminded me a little of former house speaker Nancy Lugosi without all the plastic surgeries, Botox injections, dentures, salon dyes, and hair extensions. Everything an eighty-two-year-old woman needs to look like she isn't a day over ninety-one. Compared to Glenda, and Lugosi for that matter, my old landlady Mrs. Wong was a *Baywatch* babe. I sidled up to the bar and sat down on the stool beside Glenda, noticing the glass in front of her was empty. Glenda turned to me and smiled. Her teeth looked like a dirty white picket fence with several rotten boards.

"Well... aloha, sailor. Care to buy a lady a drink?"

Confused, I glanced around the bar but didn't see anyone resembling a lady. Then, I realized what she had meant. Silly me. Glenda had referred to herself as a lady. That was a stretch. When I looked back at her, her smile had disappeared and her eyes narrowed in recognition.

"I know you. You're the crummy robbery dick who framed me. You accused me of robbing those poor servicemen and sent me up on that bogus robbery charge."

"Yes, and I remember you, Glenda. You still in the rackets?"

"No, after I got out of prison, I went straight."

"Keeping your nose clean, huh?"

"That's right Detective Bishop. You won't arrest me again. I'm clean."

"Is that so?" I didn't correct Glenda's faulty assumption that I was still a cop.

"Tell me something, Glenda. You know a guy named Joe Wang?"

"It's hard to say. It's the shakes, copper. I'm too exhausted to remember names right now. Look at this." She held up a trembling, wrinkled, and veiny hand.

"My hand is waving like I'm trying to flag down a caravan of liquor delivery trucks."

"Look, Glenda..."

"But after one or two pick-me-ups, I'm in excellent condition to remember all the names you care to know about."

"Oh, brother."

"Now, what were you saying, copper?"

"Oh, something about the evils of overindulgence. But I've forgotten now."

"In that case, maybe I'll let you buy me a drink."

"Sure."

I waved to the bartender, and he walked over.

"You want a drink, bruddah?"

I picked up Glenda's empty glass and sniffed it before replying.

"As long as you're quick about it. My companion and I don't like to wait."

"What do you want?"

"I'll have a tall, cold glass of milk and my friend here will have gin. A full bottle of gin."

"Milk?"

"Yes, with an accent on the cold. I know you have it. That guy down the bar is having a White Russian and you need milk to make those. And none of the low-fat stuff. Whole milk. I'm a guy who likes to run with the big dogs, not stay on the porch."

The bartender muttered something under his breath and then turned to get the drinks.

"You just gave me a hot flash," Glenda said, patting my left hand with her gnarled right claw.

"Okay, now do you know Joe Wang?"

The bartender brought over my milk and a bottle of cheap gin. I paid him and he went back to polishing the bar.

"Well, since you're a cop, I guess I can trust you. Besides, you're holding that lovely bottle."

"What about Wang?"

"First, how about a small glass of that truth serum? It lubricates my memory."

"First, Wang."

Glenda turned away and talked to me over her shoulder.

"Since I can't stand to look, I've turned my back on the bottle and I'll tell you what I know. Mr. Joe Wang, a very unsavory character, until his sudden arrest five years ago for gambling promotion, ran the China Doll on North Hotel Street. But he just got out of prison about a week ago and is back in Chinatown. Now, please, my mouth feels like it's stuffed with wads of cotton."

"Where does Wang live in Chinatown?"

"Ah, you are indeed a heartless rascal."

"Yeah, people say that all the time. Now spill it, Glenda."

"You aren't, by chance, a recruiter for Alcohol Anonymous?"

"You get the bottle when you tell me where to find Joe Wang."

"Bethel Street across from the Hawaii Theatre. His mother, Irene Chow, owns the place there, the Blue Goose. She runs a bar downstairs and rents rooms on the second floor. Now, please."

I twisted the cap off and poured a generous splash of gin into Glenda's glass.

"There you go."

Glenda drained the glass and smacked her lips. She wore the contented expression of a mother watching her nursing baby. I sipped my milk, waiting to see if she would tell me more about Wang.

"Ahem. As I gaze with sadness at this empty glass, I am reminded you aren't the first to come seeking the whereabouts of one Joe Wang."

"Huh? Say that again. This time in English."

"A thug, unlike you, dear sir, with the disagreeable habit of slapping my face instead of buying me a drink, approached me not an hour before you came in, seeking the same information."

"Did you give it to him?"

"I had no choice. He accosted me in the hallway when I came out of the ladies' room from which there was no escape. I had to tell him to avoid that scoundrel slapping the life out of me. He was an animal. One more slap and the delightful enjoyment of my favorite libation would have been a thing of the past."

"Did you know him?"

"No, it was my first, and hopefully last, acquaintance with that surly reprobate."

"What did he look like?"

"A large, beastly man. An Asian or Pacific Islander. Maybe Samoan. He is shading six-foot-three, with bulging biceps and a scar on his face from his right eyebrow to his jaw."

Since Glenda knew Wang, I knew I could scratch him from my list of suspects for the assault. But I wanted to know who the man was and why he was looking for Joe Wang.

"Thanks, Glenda." I slapped a twenty on the bar. "Here, buy yourself another bottle."

"Bless you," Glenda said, stuffing the twenty inside her brassiere. "Good evening to you, cousin. You're a true gentleman."

I left Glenda and the depressing bar. If you've never seen a bar like the Harbor Lounge, it's a liberal education in the misery of human beings. I felt relief breathing in the clean night air after escaping the place where the smell of stale booze was so strong, just walking inside was enough to leave you with a hangover.

It was pushing ten o'clock, and I felt dog-tired. All I wanted was to curl up in bed beside the lovely Sally Jayne Fisher and let her work her magic. But time was of the essence. Sure, I had no problem stiffing Nicole Hersey for the imaginary twenty-five hundred I'd promised. But my ex-fiancé was a woman of her word and had meant it when she said she would kick Nikki out after two nights. That meant I had more work to do tonight, or I'd wind up having to stash my personable China doll somewhere else unless I closed the case by Saturday morning. So, I hailed a cab outside of the seedy bar and rode back to Chinatown.

Chapter Nine

HAVING WORKED MANY HOMICIDES, robberies, and other assorted felonies in Chinatown when I'd been on the cops, I was intimately familiar with the district. I knew all about the Blue Goose, your typical Chinatown gun and knife club. They watered down the drinks and the rooms on the second floor, Irene rented by the hour to the customers of her hostesses. The regulars well knew Irene kept a 357-magnum next to the cash register and a 12-gauge sawed-off shotgun under the bar she would bring out from time to time.

The cabbie dropped me in front of the Hawaii Theatre. I paid him, jaywalked across Bethel Street, and strolled into the bar. For a Thursday night, the place was jumping. Given the number of sailors in the place, I figured a ship or two must have docked at Pearl and Uncle Sam had just disbursed the payroll. I had to join the five-deep line to get to the bar to speak to a bartender. There I caught the eye of a cute, tall girl with long dark brown hair wearing black tight short-shorts and a white tank and she flounced over on her high heels, latched onto my arm, and put her luscious lips next to my ear.

"You look lost, honey," she said loud enough that I could hear her over the music. "Dance with me."

She had only a little up top, which I figured was why she hadn't bothered putting on a bra. But what poked out at me from beneath the tank top's white fabric was nice to look at and went well with her slender, long brown legs and shapely bottom.

"Another time, sweetheart," I said. "I'm trying to find somebody."

The girl frowned with disappointment and stuck out her bottom lip. Then she batted her long eyelashes at me with mischief in her brown eyes.

"You will find what you want with me," she said. "Come on, let's dance."

"Later, angel. The dancing, I think you mean takes time. A long time. Don't be impatient. I have to find somebody first."

"This somebody you're trying to find. Who is it?"

"Irene Chow."

"She's not your type, baby. She's too old for you. You'll have more fun with me."

"How do I know until I try? Anyway, I'm really looking for her son."

"Oh... Joe?"

"You say his name with such tenderness, you must know him."

"I should. I'm his girl."

"Fine. Is he here?"

"He was. But he left earlier. He might come back later."

"And left you all alone? How foolish. Do you know where he went?"

"Uh-huh. But I'd get in trouble if I told you."

"Suppose I buy you a drink. Will you tell me then?"

"No. I told you. I'd get in trouble."

"Two drinks, and a fifty-dollar tip?"

The girl laughed and shook her head.

"You're nice, baby. What's your name?"

"Bishop. Rick Bishop. What's your name, honey?"

"Just call me Lucy. Your name is nice, too. Bishop. It's the same as that museum."

"Yes. it sure is. They named it after a distant ancestor of mine."

"You make me want to do something for you."

"Like telling me where Joe is?"

Lucy smiled, then bit her bottom lip.

"Unh-uh. Something else I know you would like much more."

"That sounds lovely, baby. But why won't you tell me where I can find Joe?"

"Joe's mom, Irene. She told me not to tell anybody where he is."

"Then tell me where to find Irene."

"Now, you're being impatient, baby."

"A lot of the girls like that."

Lucy laughed again. "Do they? Not me. I like it slow."

"I'll have to remember that."

"Why do you want to find Joe?"

"I've got an envelope for him."

"An envelope? Like a letter or what?"

"Something like that."

"Is it important?"

"Very. It could keep Joe from getting into trouble again."

"Oh? Why don't you give it to me? I'll see that he gets it."

"I'd love to. You're so charming. But I'm afraid I must deliver it myself."

"Suit yourself, baby. You'll find Irene upstairs. Around the corner and the third door on the right. Maybe she'll tell you where Joe is."

"Thank you, Lucy. I'll try my luck."

"If you really want to get lucky, come back and see me after you talk to Irene. Take it easy, Rick Bishop."

"I'll take it anyway that I can get it, baby."

Lucy grinned, bit her bottom lip again, and then melted into the crowd. I supposed she was looking for another customer to keep her occupied until I was available. So many beautiful girls, so little time. I had to stop working so hard.

Chapter Ten

AROUND THE CORNER FROM the restrooms, I found the stairway that led to the second floor. I shot up the stairs, taking them two at a time. I turned the corner Lucy had described and found the third door on the right. The door was open, so I walked in without knocking and there, standing in the center of the room, was the best reason I could think of for liberal immigration policies. I'd never met Irene Chow, and if the woman in the room was her, she wasn't what I had expected.

Knowing Chow had a thirty-five-year-old son, I figured she had to be on the backside of fifty, but looking at this woman, you wouldn't have guessed it. Her south of the border plus her north of the border made for some gorgeous geography. Her thick, expensively cut and styled shoulder-length dark hair framed a beautiful face with flawless skin unblemished by even a single wrinkle. I had only two criticisms. She looked like she hadn't smiled in twenty years and she had the cold, hard eyes of a woman who could probably cut your head off before you even knew you were bleeding. Since I didn't know for sure she was Irene Chow, I asked.

"Mrs. Chow?"

"She looked at me for a full minute before answering. She gave me that uneasy feeling that she could read my every thought."

"Who are you?"

"Richard Bishop. I'm looking for Joe."

"You better sit down."

I took a chair in front of a large mahogany desk. The woman walked behind me and closed the door. Then she sat down in the chair behind the desk.

"I'm Irene Chow. Ms. Chow. I'm not married. And I've never heard Joe speak of a Richard Bishop."

"No reason he should. He doesn't know me."

"What do you want with my son?"

"You might say I'm a highly paid delivery boy."

"You're making little sense, Mr. Bishop. If you're a cop, Joe did his time. Now he's tired. I'll tell no one where he is."

"Would it help any if I told you Nikki Kwan sent me?"

"Nikki Kwan, that pretentious little backstabber... Get out of here and leave Chinatown, haole. We already have enough trouble in Chinatown."

"How would you like to see Joe go back to prison?"

"I told you to get out."

"This time it would be for murder."

"If you do not go... Murder? What murder?"

I took out the sealed envelope and held it up. "Unless I deliver this to Joe. He could go back to prison for murder. And he might never get out again."

"The contents of that envelope will keep Joe from killing someone?"

"Maybe. That depends on how he likes what's in it. And I think we both know who might get killed."

"All right, Mr. Bishop. Take it to Joe. Here. I will write the address where you can find him."

Chow picked up a pen and wrote on a notepad. She tore off the page. I stood and walked to the desk and took the paper when she held it out to me. After reading the address, I folded the paper and slipped it into my jacket pocket.

"One last question, Ms. Chow. How long has Lucy Wong worked for you?"

"You know Lucy?"

"Sure, from when she used to dance over at China Doll. I hadn't seen her in a while and didn't know she was working for you."

"I see. Lucy is Joe's friend. She used to visit him in prison. And I suppose I can tell you she only started working here about a week ago."

"Yes, I understand she is Joe's girl. He's a lucky man. Lucy is an attractive woman."

"Lucy is a good girl. She earns her keep and does what I tell her. But you are mistaken. Lucy is a bar girl. I'm sure you know how she earns her living. Joe likes her, but she is only his friend... an enjoyable diversion for my son sometimes. Nothing more."

"It seems I'm misinformed. Well, thank you again, Ms. Chow. You've been very helpful. I'll show myself out."

After leaving Chow, I took the stairs back down and left the club quickly, before Lucy saw me. She was an attractive woman who I suspected might be loads of fun. And her profession didn't bother me. But I had a good thing going with a lovely blonde Australian girl that I would not ruin.

It was only a short walk to my office from the Blue Goose. I needed sleep and seeing Joe Wang could wait until morning. Besides, Lucy had told me he might return to the club, so he might not even be at the address Chow had given me. I just hoped the murder hadn't made too much of a mess in my office. The idea of sleeping in a crime scene didn't make me feel warm and fuzzy.

On the walk to my building, I pondered how Lucy Wong fitted into the picture exactly. It seemed a safe bet she probably had told Joe that Nikki Kwan had the recording and planned to hire me to deliver it to him.

Nikki hadn't told me that Lucy knew about the recording that supposedly implicated Jimmy Cho as the party who had ratted Wang out to the cops. But Lucy and Nikki had been friends and roommates, so it wasn't a stretch to believe Lucy knew about the recording. And Nikki had said that Lucy was the only person who knew she planned to hire a private investigator to deliver the recording to Wang. Lucy had even helped her find me through my website. So, the question was, had Lucy betrayed Nikki?

You could argue that Lucy telling Joe what she knew had benefited Nikki. If she had, it seemed even less likely Joe Wang would have had any reason to send Chong Pong to scare me off the case. But it might put Wang in the frame for Pong's murder. The murder was David's problem. But I was curious to find out who sent Chong Pong to my office to start with. Jimmy Cho, in the interest of self-preservation, was the obvious suspect. After I saw Joe Wang, I intended to call on Cho, if only to satisfy my curiosity. But that could wait until the morrow. My office couch, be it ever so humble, was calling to me.

Chapter Eleven

THE ALARM WOKE ME at 6:00 A.M. and I rolled out of my uncomfortable sofa bed like a fly climbing out of a bucket of molasses. I hated getting up early, but Mrs. Wong always arrived at her shop by eight. To err on the side of safety, I had to be out of the office by seven.

The previous evening, I'd arrived at my office building to find that my key no longer worked. Mrs. Wong had changed the locks. After I picked the lock on the street entrance door, I had climbed the stairs and discovered the old fusspot had taped a sheet of paper written in her shaky scrawl notifying me she had evicted me for non-payment of rent. Ignoring the warning to keep out, I had picked that lock too and let myself in.

Once inside, I had found no signs of the murder. The boys and girls from the crime lab had taken the chair I'd tied Pong to along with a large square of carpet they had cut out as evidence. I had assumed Pong had leaked blood on the carpet. Other than that, the office had looked no worse for wear. Relieved, I'd undressed, washed up, and after setting my phone's alarm, gone to sleep on the couch.

After shaving and dressing, I climbed out the window and jumped onto the fire escape, taking it down to the alley. I'd relocked both doors the night before and Mrs. Wong would be none the wiser I'd been in the office.

It was a beautiful Honolulu morning, like almost every morning when you're lucky enough to live in paradise. The sun was glowing, and it was warm, but the cool trade winds breeze made it a pleasant day for walking. Not knowing if Joe Wang was an early riser, I stopped off at a nice little café for breakfast to kill time before hot-footing it over to the address Irene Chow had given me.

Taking the most direct route from my office to the apartment house on River Street took me through the Makai Markets, an open-air market of mostly fresh fruits and vegetables. Passing some fruit stands, I felt a heavy hand on my shoulder. I looked back to see if it had an arm attached to it. It did. The arm of a very large moon-faced Asian man eating a barbecue-flavored cha siu pork bun, a Chinese-style pastry called cha siu bao in Cantonese. The pastries were available from most any bakery in Chinatown. The man was tall, but about as wide. He wore a baggy light blue Panama suit with the hat to go with it. He was stuffing the pastry in his mouth with his free hand. When he talked, his voice matched everything else about him.

"Please, Mr. Bishop. You walk too fast. I get tired easily."

"You know my name. So maybe you'd better keep talking."

"Hmm... would you like to share some of this cha siu bao?"

"No thanks. And stop spattering the barbeque sauce on my coat. Now, speak up. I'm in a hurry."

"I won't detain you long. But you have something I want."

"You're just flattering me."

"Are you sure you wouldn't like some of this cha siu bao? It's very delicious."

"No, I've already had breakfast. Now, come on, come on. What's on your mind?"

"A girl named Nikki Kwan gave you an envelope. She should have given it to me."

"Why? What do you have to do with it?"

"Please, Mr. Bishop. I told you I get tired easily."

"The man finished the pastry and continued standing in front of me, his large hand still gripping my shoulder."

"Look. You're scaring customers away from the fruit stands. Now get out of my way."

"Certainly. As soon as you give me the envelope."

"Unh-uh."

"Please don't persist in being difficult, Mr. Bishop. You might get hurt very bad. Give me that envelope."

"Okay... here..."

I slipped my right hand inside my jacket as if retrieving the envelope. Transfixed with anticipation, the guy never saw the best left hook I'd thrown in a while. After my fist connected with his jaw, I followed up with a straight right. That punch put him out like a candle flame in a stiff breeze. He fell backward into a fruit stand, crushing it under his considerable weight.

"You said you get tired easily," I said to his unconscious form. "Now you can sleep."

"Hey, mister... mister," an elderly Asian man said. "I feel very sorry for you, mister. The man you have knocked into my mango section. He is Jimmy Cho."

"It's a little late for introductions, papasan."

"Mr. Cho... he is a big man in Chinatown. And a dangerous man."

"I'll take your word for it."

"Now he lies still on top of the fruit. But watch out, mister. Because he will not lie long quiet."

I thanked the old fruit vendor for his warning and gave him forty dollars to cover the damage I'd done. Then I took a last look at Cho. He still rested comfortably. A halo of ripe, yellow mangos surrounded his fat head. I wanted to stuff one in his open mouth, but time was getting short and I had work to do. The envelope I was carrying was obviously too important to nestle in my coat pocket much longer. I threaded my way through the market, then walked through a couple of alleys, dodging some rats big enough to bark and in a few minutes knocked on what I hoped was Joe Wang's door.

Chapter Twelve

THE DOOR OPENED, FRAMING a shifty eyed guy in the doorway. He was slender, but had muscular arms with full tattoo sleeves. He had on a white wife beater with black slacks. It looked like he was having a bad hair day, with gelled spikes of close cropped dark brown hair shooting off in all directions. What was it with these guys who wore a little too much hair gel? Why couldn't they understand that a little dab will do you?

"Hello Joe."

"Your name's Bishop."

"Yes, it is. Seems like I've certainly developed quite a following in Chinatown."

My comment failed to amuse him. He gave me the faintest smile I'd ever seen.

"Yeah. Come on in."

After I entered the apartment, he closed the door.

"I didn't get the chance to ask my last admirer. But tell me. How did you know my name?"

"Never mind. Just give me the envelope."

"You're certainly a quick study. Nikki Kwan didn't say you'd know about it."

"Look, Bishop. I've just spent five years in jail. I got things to take care of. Give me the envelope."

"I might as well. It's addressed to you."

I reached into my jacket, pulled out the sealed envelope, and gave it to him. He ripped an end off it, tipped it up, and dumped the contents into his open palm. It wasn't only a simple thumb drive, as I'd expected. Instead, Joe Wang held one of those small MP3 players with a USB flash drive and a pair of white earbuds. He walked over to the sofa and sat down. Dropping the empty envelope on the coffee table, he put the earbuds into his ears and switched on the player. Since he hadn't asked me to sit, I remained standing near the front door with my arms crossed as he listened to the recording. After three or four minutes, Wang jerked the earbuds out, and tossed them with the MP3 player on the coffee table.

"That's no good," he muttered, leaning forward with his elbows on his knees and his face in his hands.

"That's not the reaction I expected," I said. "You didn't like what was on the recording?"

"All right, Bishop," he said, standing up and walking back over to me. "You've done your job. Now beat it."

"I'd like to take something back to Ms. Kwan that might make her happy. Some bright cheery word from you would do it."

"I told you to leave."

"You mean there's no reply?"

"Reply? Oh, sure, come to think of it. There is. This...."

It happened so quickly I hadn't even seen it coming. A sap maybe, or a black pipe sleeping pill. But whatever it was, he had slugged me and slugged me good on the side of the head. I went down faster than Biden's poll numbers. I tried to fight it, but it was like being on a sinking ship... trying to crawl back up the slanting deck. The ship dragged me down and the black water swallowed me up.

I must have laid on the floor for several hours. When I woke up, I could tell from the dim light coming through the blinds of a window that night was fast chasing the day away. I had a dull throbbing headache and struggled to find my way back to consciousness. I got up off the floor and looked around. Wang was gone, and so was the MP3 player. The envelope was still on the coffee table, but that did me no good. It was empty. I staggered to the door, but getting out of that apartment was like wading through an acre of glue.

Outside, I sat down on the steps, relaxed, and waited for my head to clear. Sure, I'd delivered the envelope and knew I should report to my client and collect my three-hundred-dollar bonus. But the way Wang had reacted left me feeling sure I had nothing encouraging to tell Nikki Kwan, and I wasn't ready to face her yet. Besides, my throbbing head felt as heavy as a bowling ball. I was in pain and needed someone to feel sorry for me and to nurse me back to health. And I knew just the person. A beautiful blonde at 888 Kapiolani Boulevard. Nikki Kwan would be safe at Nicole's for another night. I'd go see her tomorrow morning to give her the news. With my aching head, enduring a ninety-minute bus ride and a half dozen transfers were out of the question. So, I took out my phone and called for a cab.

Chapter Thirteen

TWENTY MINUTES LATER, I rang the bell when I arrived at Sally's condominium. Cooper opened the door.

"Hello Mr. Bishop. Come in, sir. Oh, my goodness. Mr. Bishop, you look terrible."

"It matches the way I feel. Is Ms. Fisher in?"

"Yes, sir. She's in the lounge. I'll get you an ice bag for your head, sir."

"Thanks, Cooper."

I limped into the lounge. "Hi, honey."

"Rick, Hi. Where have you been? Oh, no. You got beat up again."

"Yeah, some guy hit me on the head with something."

"Poor little baby. Come here, Ricky. Let me look at your head."

"Yes, baby. I need some sympathy and pampering."

"Oh, Rick. Your head is bloody, and there is a large bump. I better drive you to the hospital. You may have a concussion."

"That's all right, honey. I've had more concussions than an NFL quarterback and I'm a fast healer. All I need is for you to nurse me back to health."

"Aw. All right, darling. I'll have Cooper draw you a warm bath, then we can have a lie down."

"Thank you, baby."

"Mr. Bishop, here is the ice bag, sir."

"Thanks, Cooper."

"Cooper, please draw Rick a warm bath."

"Yes, madam. Right away."

After Cooper drew my bath, Sally gave me two aspirin to swallow. Then, she sat on the edge of the tub and held the ice bag to my swollen head while I soaked away all my cares in the warm water. I didn't like talking shop with Sally, but she insisted, so I told her the entire story about my case.

"So, you think the man who hit you is still going to kill your client?"

"I can't let that happen, honey. She hired me to protect her. If I let her get killed, it would be bad for my professional reputation."

"Rick, I can't stand it when you walk in all beat up. Maybe you should find another job."

"Like what?"

"Oh, I don't know. You could sell insurance or cars, something like that. You really are a talker."

"But I like my job and being my own boss, Sally. I don't want to give it up."

"Oh, I suppose."

Sally helped me out of the tub, dried me off, and wrapped me in a plush bath towel. Then she led me to her bedroom to lie down. Once she felt she had made me comfortable, she lay down beside me with her head on my chest and stroked my face tenderly.

"Rick?"

"Uh-huh?"

"Who do you love?"

"I'll never tell."

"Rick!"

"I love you, baby."

"Then let's get married."

"Uh, hey. How would you like me to sing you a little song, honey?"

"Now stop that. I want to talk about getting married."

"I think you will like this one, baby."

"Rick!"

"Again... this couldn't happen again."

"I hate you."

"This is that once in a lifetime. This is that moment divine."

"You never sing when I want you to."

"What's more, this never happened before. Though I have waited for a lifetime. That such as you would suddenly be mine... Like it, baby?"

"No."

"Mine to hold as I'm holding you now and never to part. Mine to..."

Sally climbed off the bed.

"Hey, what's the matter? Don't go."

She stood with crossed arms and glared at me.

"You want to sing? Go ahead."

"Well, what did you have in mind?"

"I'll never tell."

"You're not being very original. That's my line."

"Well, I'm mad."

"C'mere, c'mere," I said, throwing back the covers and sitting up on the edge of the bed.

"No."

I reached out for her. "Come here, honey. Please?"

Reluctantly, she walked over. I took her hands and pulled her onto my lap, and kissed her. She kissed me back and mewled a little. Then she rested her head on my chest.

"Still mad?"

"Mm, no."

"Well, let's get you mad again. It's so much fun making up."

Sally giggled. I sang again.

"Mine to have when the now and the here disappear. Again... this couldn't happen again."

"I'm mad."

"Oh, good."

We kissed some more.

"Mm... Ricky," she whimpered.

"What dear?"

"Let's lie down."

Chapter Fourteen

Sally supervised the inventory, or stock count as she called it, every Saturday morning at her surfer and beachwear boutique on Kalakaua Avenue. She offered to drop me off at Nicole Hersey's house on her way to the store. I accepted to avoid the choice between the bus and taxi fare. Neither option seemed pleasant.

As far as Sally knew, Nicole was just my attorney. Since she had brought up marriage so often lately, I thought it best to keep it that way. It seemed better that she didn't learn I'd once been engaged briefly to Nicole to avoid an argument. I enjoyed riding in her Mercedes-Benz C-Class Cabriolet convertible with the wind in my hair.

"Rick?"

"Yes, Sally baby?"

"You going to take me out tonight?"

"Sure, I'll be back at your place later. We'll have a quiet evening in."

"No, I want to go out somewhere and have a nice dinner and go dancing. If you don't take me out, I'll pout."

"Baby, I don't have the cash. I'm tapped this week and I still have to come up with last month's rent money so that petty Mrs. Wong will let me back into my office."

"Then let me take you out. I'll pay. And you know I'll give you the money to catch up on your office rent."

"No, honey. I'm not taking money from you."

"Why? The store and my trust fund provide me with plenty of money. I want to help you. I was already thinking about buying you a car for your birthday."

"Sweetheart, how could I respect myself if I took money from you? I won't be a sugar baby. I'd feel like a gigolo."

Sally laughed. "What's wrong with that? I think last night with you was well worth paying for. And you even had a sore head."

"Oh, Sally, stop being ridiculous."

"No, you stop being ridiculous, Ricky. Let me help you with your financial difficulties. I truly want to. We can even call it a loan if it makes you feel better about it."

"You know how much I appreciate the offer, baby. But no. I can't take your money or let you buy me cars or pay for our dates. Tell you what. How about we just go see an early movie and eat something at home afterwards?"

"But I want to get dressed up and to go to a nice place on a Saturday night. We haven't gone dancing for ages. I feel like we've been hibernating for months. I want to go out on the town, have a few drinks, and shake my bum a little on a dance floor."

"Why Sally!"

"Why Sally, nothing. Please, Rick?"

"I can't do it, honey. I'm broke."

I could tell from the whining and extended bottom lip, my refusal to take her out had disappointed Sally. But she took it pretty well, without a word of complaint. She wasn't speaking to me at all now. I didn't enjoy disappointing her, but I was short on funds. I'd already gone through much of the six-hundred-dollar retainer Nikki Kwan had paid me. But Sally looked so sad, and maybe even a little mad. And I was about to collect the other three-hundred. So, why not make Sally happy for once? After all, she deserved it.

"Maybe you're right, honey. We haven't been out in a while. I think I can scrape together enough for a night of dinner and dancing with the most beautiful, adorable girl in the entire world."

Sally glanced at me and smiled. "Aw, you're the sweetest man ever, Ricky. That's why I love you so much. But I was behaving selfishly. I know you haven't had many clients lately. We can stay in. Cooper can make us a nice dinner. Then we can put some music on and dance in the lounge. I know you'll take me out when you have the money."

"Honey, you always give me an argument. You never want to go anywhere. I'm tired of watching Netflix and eating hotdogs. I want to go dancing."

Sally glanced at me with a raised eyebrow. "What?"

"And I don't mean the Rendezvous Club. I want to go to the Polynesian to wine and dine my gorgeous girl and dance the night away."

"What?"

"I'm a growing boy and I want to see the bright lights and throw my money around."

"But... but, Rick... you said."

"I'll be at your place to pick you up at seven-thirty this evening, and don't even think about wearing slacks."

Sally howled with laughter. "Rick, you're an idiot."

"Right there, honey. That's the house there on the right."

Sally pulled the car to the curb and stopped in front of Nicole's house. I leaned over and gave her a long kiss that left us both a little lightheaded.

"Bye, idiot," she said with a grin. "See you later."

"Bye."

I got out of the car and walked up the sidewalk to the front door, whistling a tune as Sally drove away. I was in fine spirits and feeling fit as a fiddle after the night I'd spent with her. The headache was gone and the bump on my head had receded. And the prospect of collecting a fee always put me in a good mood. I just didn't know my mood was about to change for the worse.

I rang the doorbell, and when no one answered after several minutes, rang it again. Then I knocked on the door, but still got no response. I tried the doorknob. Locked. I heard the television going inside, but Nicole sometimes left in on when she went out to deter burglars.

Her car wasn't in the driveway, but Nicole was among the many suffering from a severe anxiety disorder that caused her to believe in nonsense like the climate change hoax. The disorder dictated she drive a Mini Cooper EV as part of her desperate attempts to help save the planet and humanity from extinction. I'd tried to coax her into therapy, but anytime I tried explaining climate change was only a natural Earth cycle that had gone on for nearly five-hundred billion years, she would shriek "denier" and foam at the mouth. So, she often parked the car in the garage since she had to charge up the stupid thing constantly. It was only a matter of time before the lithium-ion batteries malfunctioned, caught fire, and burned her house down. Realizing the amount of carbon that would put into the atmosphere would probably drive her over the edge completely.

I walked to the garage, cupped my hands, and peered through one of the glass panes at the top of the door. There was enough light coming in from the window at the back of the garage to see her car wasn't inside. Where had the girls got off to? Maybe they had gone to have breakfast somewhere, maybe to one of Nicole's favorite vegan places. I felt queasy at the thought. Why did people put themselves through stuff like that just so they could live a few years longer sitting in a wheelchair drooling in some nursing home during their senior years?

While I had my lock pick set in my wallet, I feared a neighborhood looky-loo might call the cops if they spotted me fiddling with the front door. But if the girls had gone shopping, as women are prone to do frequently, I didn't want to sit on the hard concrete front porch for hours awaiting their return. They might be gone until early afternoon. I'd much rather wait inside where I could make coffee and watch television.

At least it seemed they were getting along if they had gone out together. That might pay dividends for me. Until I determined Joe Wang's intentions toward Nikki, I needed to keep her stashed in a safe place. Maybe I could persuade Nicole to allow her to stay a few more days. Otherwise, I'd have to tap another friend for a favor. My best friend Joe Rose was probably my best bet if Nicole stuck to her two-nights only stance. Joe was single and lived alone. He never minded a gorgeous woman staying over at his place. I'd just have to remind him to keep his hands off the merchandise until I had determined my own intentions toward Nikki.

The back door seemed my best option. If Nicole had locked it, I could pick that lock without being seen by some nosy neighbor. There was a privacy fence in the back. After walking along the side of the garage to the fence, I glanced around and the coast was clear. So, I jumped, grabbed the top of the eight-foot wood fence, pulled myself up, threw my legs over the top, and dropped into the backyard. I crossed the yard, and then the patio to the back door. There I saw the one thing I hadn't expected to find. Getting inside would be no problem. Someone had broken out a pane of glass and the door stood ajar. I could see through the door broken glass on the kitchen floor.

Drawing my pistol, I pushed the door open with my foot, and entered. The television blared. There was nothing amiss in the kitchen besides the broken glass on the tile floor. I crept into the dining room, looking over the sight on the pistol. Both the dining room and living room were clear. I didn't call out in case the intruder was still inside the house.

Moving down the hallway, I ducked through the open door into the bathroom. Empty. The spare bedroom door was closed, so I passed it by and continued to the end of the hallway to the open door of Nicole's bedroom. No one was in the bedroom, en suite bathroom, or closet. Nicole had made the bed, assuming she'd slept in it the previous night. I saw nothing suggesting a burglary. All the electronics were present. Nicole's jewelry box seemed undisturbed. No one had opened or dumped any drawers. Taking a deep breath, I moved back into the hallway. I had only the spare bedroom left to clear. I turned the knob and then shoved the door open with my gun at the ready.

Chapter Fifteen

THE ROOM WAS EMPTY except for the sleeping woman lying on her back on the bed with the covers pulled up to her chin. With a feeling of relief, I holstered the gun. I couldn't believe Nikki was sleeping through the sound of the blaring television in the living room, especially now after I'd opened the bedroom door. The lights were off, but there was enough sunlight coming through the half-closed window blinds to see the peaceful expression on Nikki's pretty face. It seemed a shame to wake her. Maybe she and Nicole had stayed up late drinking wine. But we needed to talk. I flipped on the overhead light before approaching the bed to avoid startling her. I crossed the room to the bed, put a hand on her shoulder, and gave it a gentle shake.

"Wake up sleepy head," I whispered.

Nikki's eyes didn't open and with the light on, I saw her face seemed paler than I'd remembered. I got a sick feeling in my stomach as I understood why she looked so peaceful. Nikki Kwan could stop being afraid of dying. I pressed my fingers to the side of her neck to check for a pulse to make certain, but I already knew she was gone. Carefully, I pulled back the covers. Blood soaked the front of her pajama top, but there hadn't been enough blood to soak through the comforter. The handle of a carving knife protruded from her chest. That seemed the only wound.

The knife had probably gone right through her heart. The amount of blood suggested it had stopped pumping quickly, so she probably went fast. She might have been asleep when stabbed and might not have even woken up or felt pain for more than an instant. As far as violent deaths, I'd seen much worse. Still, as many homicide victims as I'd seen, I'd never got used to it. Like now, the first look always upset my stomach. My mouth filled with saliva and I had to keep swallowing until my stomach settled.

In a daze, I walked out and back into the living room. I switched off the television. Then I wondered where Nicole Hersey was? I walked into the kitchen, where I knew Nicole kept a wooden knife block. One knife was missing, and the others had the same handles as the knife in Nikki's chest. I checked the dishwasher to confirm the knife missing from the block wasn't in there. The dishwasher was empty.

Questions filled my tortured mind. Why wasn't Nicole at home? Had the women had a falling out? I didn't want to have the thoughts I was having about a close friend, but the murder weapon came from Nicole's kitchen. Who knew what a person caught up in climate change hysteria was capable of? It had all the hallmarks of a sick cult. The true believers like Greta Thunberg, the mentally troubled little Scandinavian, differed little from those poor souls caught up in the Heaven's Gate Cult who committed mass suicide in 1997 after the cult leaders convinced them they were all going to hitch a ride on the Hale-Bopp comet. The anxiety ridden youth were always the easy marks for the diabolical, money-grubbing climate change charlatans like Al Gore.

Maybe Nicole had grown fond of Nikki and caught in the web of her psychosis believed she was saving a friend from the horrors of an imagined climate change doomsday. Had it been a twisted mercy killing? I still recalled how upset Nicole had been the day she told me she had learned on cable news the oceans were rising at an alarming rate of 63/1000th of an inch per year, as though she couldn't fathom how tiny an amount it was, much less how laughable the idea that a bloated federal agency even possessed the capacity to measure something that minuscule from space. Where was my friend and former fiancé now? On the run? On a plane bound for some third world country without an extradition treaty? Or had she looked at her bloody hands and come to grips with the horror of what she had done and driven to Halona Blowhole and thrown herself into the ocean to avoid life in prison?

When I turned to the breakfast bar, I saw it next to the coffee maker. It was a note. Tears of relief flooded my eyes as I read it. It was a note Nicole had left for Nikki that morning telling her she had gone to the office for a few hours, but would be home by lunchtime. There was also a postscript where Nicole reminded Nikki to call me since the two-night agreement had expired. That seemed a little harsh, but at least I knew my friend wasn't a stone-cold killer.

After wiping my eyes and blowing my nose on a paper towel, I took out my phone and called David Chang. I called his cell phone since I knew he didn't work on Saturdays. Today, he would have to make an exception.

The doorbell rang. I went to the front door and opened it.

"Hello, Rick."

"Nice of you to show up, Lieutenant Chang. I only called you an hour ago."

"Yes, I know you said it was important. But I was on the sixth hole at the Royal Hawaiian and was sharing a cart. I had to hike back to the clubhouse, stow my clubs, and get my car."

"Never mind the excuses, Lieutenant Chang. Follow me, please."

I turned and walked through the hallway to the spare bedroom where Nikki lay in situ.

"Why so formal, Rick?" David said. "Are you mad... Holy smoke! Where did you get that stiff?"

"I didn't get her. I inherited her."

"Neat job, Rick. Stabbed. Right through the heart. Who did it?"

"My guess is somebody with a knife."

"Hilarious," David said, walking over for a closer look. "You touch anything?"

"I only lifted the comforter after checking for a pulse and determining she was dead."

"Looks like a kitchen carving knife."

"Brilliant deduction, Holmes. And it came from the knife block in the kitchen of this house."

"Yes, right through the heart. It stopped pumping almost as soon as they stabbed her, judging from the amount of blood."

"Aren't you going to ask who she is?"

"Don't need to. I know her. Michelle Bai."

"Some detective you are, David. That isn't her name. That's my client Nikki Kwan."

"No, Rick. That might be the name she gave you, but that's Michelle Bai all right. Five years ago, she wasn't only Joe Wang's girlfriend, she was his right-hand girl."

"His right-hand girl?"

"In his gambling operations. She was in it up to her ears. By sheer luck, she wasn't on the ship the night the vice squad raided it. We brought her in later, but the county prosecutor decided we didn't have enough to charge her, so we had to let her go."

"You sure about all that, David?"

"Positive. You ever play the lottery?"

"Lottery?"

"One of Chinatown's oldest rackets. Everybody down there plays it. Strictly under cover, of course."

"Was Nikki... I mean, Michelle mixed up with the lottery?"

"Mixed up in it? She ran the entire lottery works after Joe Wang expanded into the boat casino business. Funny thing happened with that lottery... funny thing..."

"Don't keep me waiting, David. I'm dying for a laugh."

"The night vice raided the boat, they simultaneously hit China Doll, Joe's nightclub. Vice caught them red-handed. When they served the warrant, Wang's people were printing lottery tickets when the vice boys walked in. That's why the county got the boat and the club with civil asset forfeiture and Wang's house. They wiped him out."

"Why didn't they prosecute Bai for the lottery part of it? You said she ran the whole thing."

"Vice was sure she was running the lottery operation for Joe Wang, but she wasn't at China Doll that night either. She wasn't on the island. She had gone back to Hong Kong to visit relatives. We didn't pick her up until a week later when she arrived at the airport. We always wondered if someone had tipped her to the raids in advance and she had got out of harm's way until it was all over. Anyway, we didn't have enough to make any charges stick against her."

"Was she the one that tipped vice and helped take Wang out of circulation?"

"We never knew. And neither did Wang. He got violent at his trial. Kept screaming he'd get whoever had squealed on him."

"This is like a nightmare."

"Say, isn't this your ex-fiancé's house? What's her name? Nicole?"

"Nicole Hersey. Yes, this is her house."

"Huh? It's her house, and probably her knife. Do you think..."

"No, David. There's a note on the breakfast bar that should give her an alibi. You can call her law office to verify it. The note says she went there to work for a few hours this morning, but she should be back within the hour."

"I had to ask. Bai was your client, and she was an attractive woman and I've known you for a long time, Rick. With a good-looking woman you might have some recent history with, lying dead in your ex-fiancé's house, it just makes sense to consider the jealousy murder angle."

"She was only a client, David. I wasn't sleeping with her. You can forget any jealousy murder angle. Nicole was kind enough to let Nikki... Michelle, I mean, stay here for a couple of nights to keep her safe. That's the entire story. And someone, probably the killer, forced entry through the back door. That's how I got in when I arrived. They left the door ajar."

"Okay, I better call Sergeant Rowden and get the crime lab people out here."

"Sure thing, David. Make yourself at home. Nicole should be back from the office anytime now."

I turned to walk out of the room.

"Come back here, Rick. I want to ask you some more questions."

"I'll see you later, David. When I've got some answers."

"Don't you start that again. Let me tell you something. You've got that look in your eyes, the look that always ties my stomach in knots. And, I have got no Alka-Seltzer with me. I'm warning you..."

"Hey, David."

"Oh, what is it, Rick?"

"Bye."

Chapter Sixteen

I WAITED IMPATIENTLY IN front of the house for the taxi I'd called for to arrive. I wanted to be away before Nicole got home. She would blame me for Nikki bleeding all over the bed in the spare bedroom, as if I had anything to do with it. She was the one who had agreed to take in a woman with a death threat hanging over her head. That hadn't been smart of Nicole. But she would probably demand I pay to replace the mattress and bedding, even though it was all her own fault. And right now, I needed no more drama. I had enough on my plate already. Finally, the taxi arrived, and we headed to Chinatown.

While I wasn't happy that Nikki Kwan, aka Michelle Bai, had lied to me, I had been fond of the girl and she hadn't deserved to die. And with my client dead and unable to pay me the bonus she owed me for delivering the envelope to Wang, I figured someone in Chinatown owed me three hundred bucks. And Joe Wang was the first person I intended to see about it. I also wanted to find out if he'd made good on his threat by killing Michelle Bai. Another question I wanted answered was why Joe and his mother Irene Chow hadn't bothered to tell me Michelle's true name. It had been obvious they both knew who I was talking about when I had mentioned the name Nikki Kwan to them.

Gray, two-story apartment buildings lined the street Wang lived on. To the outsider, the area might seem decrepit, but it reminded me of why I'd always loved Chinatown. This was still the old Hawaii, a commercial and residential district in the heart of downtown Honolulu where, with few exceptions, most of the two- and three-story buildings dated to 1900, built after a large fire had razed the district that year. Chinatown had kept its historic buildings and its identity as a thriving Asian community over the years, surviving the influx of money and smoked glass windows that defined much of the rest of Honolulu.

Taking the stairs to the second floor, I knocked on the dark green door painted many years ago. But after knocking until my knuckles hurt, Wang didn't open the door. I tried the knob and found it locked. My enthusiastic knocking had drawn several neighbors to their doors to see what all the fuss was about. I couldn't pick the lock with all the witnesses around watching and knew it would be pointless to ask any of them if they had seen Wang around. Sure, I was a native Hawaiian, born and raised in Honolulu, but to these people I was just another imperialist haole shamus they wouldn't give the time of day to. It occurred to me, Wang might be at the Blue Goose visiting his girlfriend, Lucy. It was worth going down there. Even if I didn't find Wang, I wanted to ask Irene Chow a few questions.

I hadn't even made it a block before Nicole Hersey began blowing up my phone with calls and text messages. Evidently, she had arrived home on her own or Lieutenant Chang had summoned her there. I wasn't in the mood to chat with Nicole, so I turned the phone off before pocketing it.

Even though I no longer considered her a suspect in Michelle Bai's murder, I hoped David would put her on ice for a while by taking her to the station for questioning. I hadn't believed for a second that I'd convinced him to forget the jealousy killing angle. David had always preferred the path of least resistance in homicide investigations.

It worried me that if I kept ignoring her calls and texts, Nicole might show up at Sally's door later. I hadn't told her about Sally, but Nicole had always been a little stalkerish towards me. It wouldn't have surprised me to learn she might have tailed me to Sally's place and discovered I had a new girl. If Nicole showed up there and caused a scene, it might drag the whole engagement thing out into the open. That was the last thing I wanted to happen.

It was about a forty-minute walk from Joe Wang's apartment to the Blue Goose, but it was another beautiful morning and I had to save my pennies for my date with Sally. Since I hadn't collected the bonus, that would exhaust the last of my meager funds, but a promise was a promise. So, resolved to walk it, I set off for the Blue Goose at a brisk pace. But as I turned a corner onto Waimanu Street, I had a quick change of heart.

"That's far enough, Bishop."

"Well, look what I've picked up. And your company is about as welcome as a wad of gum stuck to the sole of my shoe."

"All right, comic, into that alley."

"Why don't you put that cannon away? It sticks out like a fly on a wedding cake."

"Hurry and get going."

"I can run if it would help."

"No, you better take your time. You don't have much of it left."

"Stop poking me. You've got a cold barrel."

"You don't like it?" he asked, shoving me in the back with his left hand.

The shove told me he held the gun in his right hand. So, as we entered the alley, I said, "No... but it helps..." Then I spun on the balls of my feet to the right suddenly, trapped his right arm against my body in the crook of my left arm while simultaneously shooting my right arm past his head and putting pressure against his neck with my right upper arm. Having him locked up and off balance, I kneed him three quick times in the gut, knocking the wind out of him. Then I rotated further to the right, grabbed the gun barrel with my right hand and pulled up while pushing down on his wrist with my left. After I ripped the gun out of his hand, I spun right again, facing him. I shoved him hard in the chest with my left hand while backing away three steps with the gun pointed in a two-handed grip at his chest. I'd practiced that old gun in the back technique a million times back in my Navy SEAL team days. The shove had put him on his can on the pavement.

"That was a little demonstration of the manly art of self-defense. Next time, don't get so close with a gun."

I had never seen the guy, but I recognized him from Glenda's description. He was a big guy, a Pacific Islander, with bulging biceps and an angry scar running from his right eyebrow to his jaw.

"Okay, so I got a little careless, shamus. You've got the gun now. What are you going to do?"

"Maybe I'll shoot you. I've got a mean streak, and it shows up whenever someone tries to kill me. I'm going to ask a couple of questions. If you don't answer them, you'll wish you have picked on another old lady. Now get up."

The guy groaned as he got shakily to his feet.

"My, you are a big boy, aren't you?"

"Big enough to break you in half, cousin."

"That supposed me to make me turn pale? The guy that gave you that scar is the one I'd worry about, not you. Step back until your back is against that wall."

As the hood shuffled backwards, I took a few steps forward.

"Now, who sent you after me?"

"I don't know his name."

I rapped him on the side of the head with the barrel of the large frame revolver.

He gasped and staggered.

"I don't know, I told you."

I slapped him again. "Who sent you after me?"

"Honest, I don't know."

I tagged him with the gun barrel a third time, only a little harder.

"No, wait... just wait a second," he groaned. "Don't hit me again. I'll tell you what I know."

"Make it fast. I'm feeling twitchy and growing fond of bouncing this gun barrel off your thick skull."

"The guy called me on the phone. Said his name was... uh... Li."

"Sure, Li is in the top three most common Chinese family names on the planet. It's sort of like saying Smith or Jones."

"Wait... wait... I know it sounds phony, but I've worked for him before and he always pays well and in advance. He leaves an envelope with the cash with a grocer in my neighborhood for me to pick up. That's why I've never seen him, just talked to him on the phone."

"How much did you get for this job?"

"Uh... five hundred. Only this time I get paid after the job."

"Okay, next question. Who killed Michelle Bai?"

"I don't know any Michelle Bai."

I backhanded him with the gun barrel on the other side of the head. "I thought you had got over being stubborn."

The guy moaned and shook his head to clear it.

"You seem a little slow, so I'll word the question differently. Who killed Michelle Bai?"

"It wasn't me, bruddah. But that's all I'm saying. I'll take the beating."

"Okay, let's try an easier question. Did this Mr. Li send you to the Harbor Lounge a couple of nights ago to get some information from a drunk lady?"

"How do you know about that?"

"I'm good at guessing games. Now, I guess you've told me all you're going to. I'm going to let you go. But before I walk away, I'm going to pat you down to make sure you have no other weapons. Turn around and assume the position on the wall. I'm sure a smart guy like you knows how to do it."

The man turned slowly, put his hands on the wall of the building, and then took a step back and spread his feet apart.

"I've got nothing else. I only had that gun."

Taking the gun by the barrel, I slugged him behind the ear with the gun butt and put him to sleep.

"Maybe that will teach you to pick on an old lady."

Reaching into his coat, I found his wallet and pulled it out. His Hawaii driver's license identified him as John Mageo. Inside the wallet were five crisp one-hundred-dollar bills. I guessed he had been lying about getting paid after the job. And since I'd done all the work, it seemed only fair that I got the money. I stuck the bills into my pocket. There were also two lottery tickets with Chinese symbols on them in his wallet. I supposed that was what David had told me about. I let him keep those. Maybe he'd get lucky and win his five hundred back. But the lottery tickets gave me an idea about who wanted me dead.

After taking a photo of his license with my phone in case I needed to visit with him again, I put the wallet back inside his coat pocket. Then an idea occurred to me, so I checked Mageo's other pockets and found his phone. I shoved the gun down inside the front of his pants. Then I used his phone to call 911. I told the operator a big man with a scar on his face was waving a gun around. After I gave her the address for the alley, I hung up. After putting the phone back where I'd found it, I left Mageo to finish his nap. I hadn't even made it a half a block before I heard the sirens.

Chapter Seventeen

FOR SOME REASON, I never seem to get where I'm going. After leaving Mageo, a restaurant caught my eye as I passed. It reminded me I was hungry, so I stopped for lunch. While eating, I realized I needed to untangle the bundle of nerves I'd become since discovering my murdered client. Now I had no client and no case. No one was paying me to solve the murder of Michelle Bai. That was the responsibility of the Honolulu cops. And I was two hundred dollars ahead of where I'd expected to be at the end of the case. So, did I really need to see Joe Wang or Irene Chow? Did I need to keep sticking my nose into something that was no longer my business until some Chinatown thug cut it off for me? Sometimes you have to turn mother's picture to the wall and get out when you can't come up with any reason that make sense to keep beating your head against a brick wall. Besides, I had a date with a beautiful blonde and needed some clothes for our night out on the town.

There were some clean clothes back at my building, but I didn't feel like breaking into my office again. And it would be risky anyway, while Mrs. Wong's herbal shop was open for business. So, I left the restaurant and took a cab to my favorite clothes shopping venue.

At the Goodwill store on South Beretania Street, you could find clothing bargains that would blow your mind. Wealthy people bought new clothes they didn't need all the time. Once their closets got full, naturally, they donated a lot of nice garments to Goodwill. They got the chance to feel virtuous for ten minutes and got a tax deduction to boot that helped them avoid paying Biden's idea of their fair share. Guys like me got the opportunity to pick up some high quality, gently used garments with a lot of wear left in them at super low prices.

After picking up a nice summer weight navy suit, a shirt, genuine silk tie, and a pair of shoes in my size that looked almost brand new, I was all set for my date with Sally. Best of all, I paid less than thirty-five bucks for the entire outfit. But I was a discriminating Goodwill shopper. I drew the line at buying used underwear and socks. But I needed those too, so I walked two blocks down South Beretania to a chain pharmacy store and picked up a new pair of socks and a package of underwear. A few toiletries completed my shopping needs. Then I walked over to my gym on Kona Street to use the shower facilities.

Technically, it wasn't my gym. I had little spare time for fitness activities other than some occasional jogging or swimming at the beach. And those activities were free. But I stopped by the gym whenever I had the chance to flirt with Angela, an attractive personal trainer who worked there. Angela had grown a little fond of me, and gave me the door code so I could get inside to use the showers whenever I wanted.

Lucky for me, Angela was off on Saturdays. If she'd seen me all dressed up in my new outfit, she would have known I had a hot date for the evening. She wouldn't have liked it. Angela had a jealous streak, and a mean streak to go with it. And I wasn't in the mood to get used as a punching bag by an angry woman who taught kick boxing.

It was 2:00 P.M. when I walked out of the gym, showered, shaved, and with my perfectly coiffed hair. I was the man about town in my sleek new suit and looked and felt like a million bucks. It was still too early to head to Sally's place, so I flagged down a bug-eyed cabbie to take me to see my best friend, Joe Rose. Joe and I had served together in the SEAL teams. Now he owned one of the nicest bars off Waikiki, the Likelike Club. I needed to talk a little business with Joe, anyway.

Chapter Eighteen

THE CABBIE DROPPED ME off at the club ten minutes later and I went inside. Joe was sitting on a stool in his usual place at the corner of the bar. And he wasn't alone. To my surprise, David Chang sat at the bar beside him. They both turned and looked at me when I walked in.

"Richard," Joe said. "Long time, no see."

"We both know why I haven't been in here in a while, Joe."

"Well, don't worry. Koko isn't here. She took the weekend off to go to Maui with her boyfriend."

"That's the best news I've heard all day."

Koko Mahelona, Rick's bar manager and partner, was another ex-girlfriend. She was a sweet kid, and I was very fond of her. But when we were dating, all she had ever wanted to talk about was marriage and having my babies. We had broken up after Koko found out I'd accidentally slept with her best girlfriend, Gabby Inouye. Koko had taken the breakup harder than I had, and she had pressured Joe to ban me from the Likelike whenever she was working.

"Rick, where the devil have you been?" David asked. "I tried to call you a dozen times and your phone has been off."

"Yeah, sorry, David," I said, taking a seat on the stool between him and Joe. "I had to turn it off because Nicole Hersey was blowing up my phone all morning."

Moki, the bartender, put a bottle of Longboard lager on the bar in front of me.

"Mahalo, Moki."

"Sure thing, Rick."

"Boy, I wouldn't want to be you when that woman gets her hands on you," David said. "She was mad enough to eat nails when she got home this morning. If you had still been there, I would have had two bodies on my hands."

"Like any of that was my fault," I said. "Women always twist things around. Anyway, have you made any progress in finding out who killed Michelle?"

"No, I don't have a single lead on that one. But I arrested the guy who killed that Chong Pong in your office, and, in the process, solved two other murders."

"Well, congratulations, David. How did you manage all that?"

"It was a funny thing. Dispatch received an anonymous 911 call about a man waving a gun around in an alley off Waimanu Street. When the patrol officers arrived, they found a guy fitting the description lying unconscious in the alley. They said someone had worked him over pretty well."

"How terrible. Is the guy going to be okay?"

"Yeah fine. He only had a mild concussion. Anyway, they checked him to see if he had a gun while they were waiting for the ambulance to arrive and found a revolver on him. The lab did routine ballistics tests on it and discovered it was the same gun used in two unsolved murders."

"Huh? But how did that solve the Chong Pong murder?"

"Sergeant Rowden interrogated the guy, John Mageo, when we got him to the station from the hospital. Mageo cracked and not only confessed to the two unsolved murders, he admitted to Rowden he had also shot Chong Pong with his own gun in your office. He said a guy named Li paid him to do it to frame you."

"Rowden broke the case?" I asked in astonishment.

"He sure did."

"Well, I guess the idiom is true."

"What idiom, Rick?"

"Even a blind hog finds an acorn once in a while."

"Oh, Rick. You need to lay off Rowden. He isn't a bad guy. For a hammerhead."

"Who's Rowden?" Joe asked.

"He's a stupid sergeant that works for David," I said.

"What's wrong with him?"

"Besides being stupid? He looks like Lurch and has the biggest feet of any guy I've ever seen. His shoes are so big, every time I see them I get the urge to smash champagne bottles on them to launch them."

Joe laughed at that one and while David tried not to, he joined in.

"Why are you so dressed up, anyway?" David asked me.

"I've got a big date tonight with a gorgeous blonde. We're going out for dinner and dancing."

"Now, Rick. You've got a pretty good thing going with Sally Fisher," David said. "You sure you want to risk messing that up?"

"David, I'm surprised at you. Sally is the gorgeous blonde I'm talking about. I'm taking her out for a night on the town."

"Oh, all right then. I just never know with you, Rick. You chase so many blondes around town I can't keep track of them."

"Not to mention the brunettes and redheads," Joe chimed in.

"Don't you start Joe," I said. "Or I won't let you loan me the money."

"What money?"

"Crazy old Mrs. Wong evicted me again just because I fell a little behind on the rent. And I'm tapped out at the moment."

"To be fair, Rick, the murdered guy in your office was the final straw for Mrs. Wong," David said. "That's why she evicted you."

"Well, all I know is I need a cash infusion fast to get back into her good graces. Without access to my office, I'm probably losing potential clients left and right and have no place to do my laundry."

"Well, I'm not loaning you any money, Richard," Joe said. "You never get around to paying me back when I do. Besides, I'm running a bar, not a saving and loan."

"I can't believe you, Joe. After all that I've done for you. And I'm your best friend."

"Oh, all right. I guess I can let you have a couple of hundred bucks as long as you swear you will pay it back this time."

"I need a little more than that, Joe."

"What? How much?"

"Well, I need a thousand to pay Mrs. Wong last month's rent. And knowing her, she will insist on getting at least half of this month's rent to go with it before she'll let me back in my office. So, fifteen hundred should do it. And you know I'm good for it. Just as soon as the insurance company pays off the claim on my car, I'll pay you back."

"Oh, yeah? When do you expect them to pay your claim?"

"Any day now. Nicole is pushing them hard."

"You mean Nicole Hersey?" David asked. "She's still your lawyer?"

"Of course. Just because the engagement didn't work out, doesn't mean we can't still be good friends and business associates."

"In that case, you better call her and smooth things over, Rick. That woman wants your scalp."

"All right, Richard," Joe said. "Against my better judgement, I'll loan you the fifteen hundred. But I'm warning you, pal. You better pay me back this time and within a reasonable time."

"I promise, Joe. You want me to pinky swear?"

"No, I'll pass on that. You want me to go to the office and get the money out of the safe now?"

"No, I don't want to walk around with that kind of cash on me tonight while I'm out wining and dining Sally. I'll come by tomorrow to pick it up and then I can square things with that old bat, Mrs. Wong, Monday morning."

"Hey wait a minute. If you're so broke, how do you have money to take your girlfriend out on the town?" Joe asked.

"Oh, I'm not paying," I lied. "Sally is. She's a trust baby."

"You should be ashamed, Rick," David said. "Asking your girlfriend to pay for the date."

"She insisted on it, David. You know how women are. They tell you what to do and you do it if you know what's good for you."

"Well, why don't you get the fifteen hundred from her?" Joe asked.

"Because I have my pride, Joe. I'm not asking my girlfriend for a loan."

"It didn't bother you to put the bite on me."

"That's different, Joe. We aren't dating."

"At least that's something I can be thankful for."

"Hey, Rick," David said. "I've been meaning to ask you. Did you ever find Joe Wang?"

"Yeah, Glenda told me how to find him."

"So, you got some information out of her, huh?"

"Yes, Glenda is a lousy drunk but a sweet kid. I bought her a bottle of cheap gin, and she sang like a nightingale."

"Well, what did he say when you gave him that recording? Did it change his mind? I want to know if he's good for the Michelle Bai killing."

"Don't you know?"

"No, how could I? You haven't told me what he said when you gave him that recording. You took off from Hersey's house this morning like you were running from a yard full of snakes."

"That's silly, David."

"What's silly?"

"There aren't any snakes in Hawaii."

"That's an urban legend, Rick. Haven't you heard of island blind snakes and yellow-bellied sea snakes?"

"Well, okay. Point taken. But what you said is still silly. You couldn't find a yard full of snakes in Hawaii if your life depended on it."

"I know that. It's just a saying. Hey, wait a minute. You stop that right now."

"Stop what, David?"

"You know what. You're doing it again. Another of those stupid routines just to confuse me. Every time I ask you a question, you get me off on some tangent like this snake nonsense. Now be serious for a second. Will you?"

"David, I'm surprised at you."

"Surprised at what?"

"You're a police detective."

"What the blazes does that have to do with anything?"

"You were a rookie once, weren't you?"

"Of course I was."

"You worked your way up to detective sergeant and then to head of the criminal investigation division, didn't you?"

"You know good and well I did."

"Wasn't it a little tough?"

"You bet it was. I patrolled a beat for four long years before I made detective. I did it by the sweat of my brow... Now wait a minute! How did we get into this?"

"You started it."

"I did?"

"Yes, David. You asked me about Joe Wang."

"Oh, yeah... Oh, I knew it. I knew it. You conniving, underhanded louse. You always do this to me. I'll bet you sit around at night pulling the wings off of flies for laughs."

"Moths."

"All right, moths. You sit around thinking up little games to pull on the police department, and you use me like... like..."

"A comic foil?"

"Yeah, I was going to say the butt of your stupid jokes. But yeah, a comic foil. And I'm tired of it. Bishop, for once I'm going to find out what's at the end of the merry-go-round. Now, I want to know what Joe Wang told you when you handed over that recording."

Kidding around with David was a sport for me. And whether he would admit it or not, he got a kick out of it too. But I'd let up on him once he started sounding a little upset. When that happened, I knew it was time to lay off and get serious.

"Oh, all right, David. You don't have to get sore. He said little of anything. But I got a strong impression it might not have changed his mind about carrying out his threat."

"What makes you say that?"

"Oh, I suppose it was the way he sapped me and left me lying unconscious on the floor of his house for several hours. He'd gone by the time I woke up, so I didn't get the chance to ask him to elaborate."

"Huh? Interesting. That makes me think I better send Rowden and a couple of squad cars to pick him up and haul him in for questioning. What's his address?"

I gave David the address. "Can you wait until Monday to pick him up, David?"

"Why?"

"He isn't going anywhere. And I want to talk to him again to clear something up."

"Clear what up? Your client is dead. You no longer have a case."

"That's true, but since someone killed Michelle, I never got paid for delivering that recording. So, the way I see it, someone owes me the three hundred bucks I earned for doing it. I want to talk to Joe Wang about it and see if he's willing to pay me. He can't do that if he's sitting in jail."

"You sure he won't leave Honolulu?"

"Why would he? You haven't talked to him yet. He's not an official suspect. Besides, I think he depends on his mother, Irene Chow, for support until he gets back on his feet after his prison stretch."

"Oh, all right. I'll give you until noon on Monday to collect your money, Rick. But then I'm having Rowden pick him up."

"Fair enough."

I looked at the clock. Moki had kept putting another beer in front of me every time I finished one, and I'd lost track of how many I'd had. I didn't want to show up drunk to pick up Sally.

"Hey, Moki."

"Yeah, Rick?"

"Can you call me a taxi, please?"

"You got it, cousin."

"Leaving already?" Joe asked.

"Yes, I better get over to Sally's place and see what's cooking. But I'll be in tomorrow afternoon sometime to pick up the money."

"Okay, Richard. But I mean it. I expect you to pay me back this time."

"Don't worry, Joe. I'm sure I'll get that insurance settlement any day now."

I heard a car horn out front.

"That's my cab, guys."

After saying so long to my pals, I left the bar.

Chapter Nineteen

I ARRIVED AT SALLY's condominium early, but that was okay. She was always glad to see me and it would give me the chance to drink some coffee to counteract the beer. Cooper opened the door when I rang the bell.

"Oh, it's you, Mr. Bishop. Come in, sir. We weren't expecting you until seven-thirty."

"Yes, I know, Cooper. But I finished work early today, so here I am. Is Ms. Fisher in?"

"Yes, sir. She is in her bedroom getting dressed. Please make yourself comfortable in the lounge. I'll let Ms. Fisher know you're here."

"Thank you, Cooper. Any chance I could get a cup of coffee?"

"Certainly, sir. Cream or sugar?"

"No, just black."

"Yes, sir."

I walked into the living room and sat down on the sofa while Cooper went to announce me and get the coffee.

I'd finished one cup of coffee and Cooper had just given me a refill when Sally swept into the room. She looked ravishing in a red sleeveless V-neck cocktail dress with a ruffled tulip hem.

"Hi, Sally baby," I said. "You look stunning in that dress."

"Hi," she said, pirouetting to give me the full view. "Like it?"

"I love it, gorgeous."

"My, aren't you the eager boy? You're early."

"Yes, I simply couldn't bear spending another minute away from you, my love."

"Oh? That's so sweet of you, darling. Hey. Look at you. A new suit. Isn't that an Armani? Very nice and it looks so good on you."

"This old thing? Yes, it is an Armani. You know my motto. Dress sharp. Look sharp."

"Oh, is that your motto? You must have forgotten to mention it before. I thought you said you're broke, Ricky. Where did you get the money for an expensive new suit?"

"Well, I took your advice, dear."

"Advice? What advice."

"You told me being a gigolo was nothing to be ashamed of. So, it's my new side gig. I was busy working all morning at the hotels down on Waikiki and made enough in tips to buy this suit."

"Oh, you did not, you idiot. And I'm sure that wasn't what I said exactly."

"I must have misunderstood."

"Where are you taking me?"

"The Polynesian, dear. We have an eight o'clock reservation."

"Shall I drive us?"

"Oh, no, baby. With the evening I have planned, neither of us will be in any condition to operate heavy machinery by the end of the night. I want to eat a nice steak and have too much to drink when we're not moving our feet around the dance floor."

"Oh? Sounds lovely. Then I'll have Cooper drive us and we can take a taxi home."

With our plans made, I helped Sally with her wrap, and Cooper drove us to the nightclub.

After the most enjoyable Saturday evening we'd spent together in a long while, Sally and I, both a little tipsy, had gone back to her place. After dancing most of the night away, we spent the rest of it together. That had been even more fun than our night out on the town. It had also been more strenuous than the dancing, so we had slept late Sunday morning. Then after brunch, I had kissed Sally goodbye and had gone to meet Joe at the Likelike to get the money he had agreed to loan me. I had returned to Sally's condo and spent Sunday night. Then, bright and early on Monday morning, I'd taken a taxi to my office building to negotiate with Mrs. Wong.

Recalcitrant as always, at first Mrs. Wong had insisted she no longer wanted me as a tenant. But when I pulled out the fifteen portraits of Franklin in a lovely shade of green and waved them around, the old battle axe had looked at the money like a fat lady eyeing a French pastry. Eventually, she had relented, and taken the fifteen hundred. She agreed to let me back in the office, providing I paid the other half of the current month's rent before the end of the month, along with reimbursing her for replacing the carpeting that the crime lab gang had cut up. I didn't know how I would come up with the money by the end of the month, but had agreed to her terms. I had no other choice.

By nine o'clock Monday morning, with a key to the new locks in my pocket, I was back in my office drinking coffee and doing some laundry. Once I had a load on the clothesline drying and another soaking in the sink, I left the office and walked to Joe Wang's apartment. All the way there, a little voice kept telling me not to go, but I knew I couldn't live with myself if I didn't find out who had killed my client, Michelle Bai. I thought I owed her that much. And from almost any angle, Joe Wang looked good for her murder. I was halfway up the stairs to Wang's apartment before I heard it.

Chapter Twenty

I COULD FEEL THE goosebumps growing, big as hailstones and twice as cold. It was a woman's voice, wailing and sobbing, a voice filled with hopelessness and grief. I hesitated for a moment and then continued up the stairs towards the sound of the voice.

When I reached the apartment's open door, I saw something I'd never forget. In the middle of the floor sat Irene Chow, her face twisted into a terrifying mask. With glazed eyes and her lips set in a thin, hard line that barely moved as she sobbed, she rocked back and forth. And stretched out full length on the floor, his head resting in Irene's lap, was Joe Wang. There was a big splotch of blood on the chest of his white wife beater shirt.

Crossing the room, I knelt down beside Irene. She looked up at me with tear-filled eyes.

"He is dead. My son Joe is dead."

"I'm sorry for your loss, Ms. Chow," I whispered.

"When Joe came home from prison, I was so happy. Now my life is black."

"Ms. Chow... who killed Joe?"

"I do not know. He came to me last night, and was upset. But he would not tell me what was the matter. Then he left. I called him all day Sunday, but he did not answer. I came here this morning. When he didn't open the door, I let myself in with a spare key and found him like this."

"Last week I gave Joe a recording."

"A recording?"

"Yes, that's what was in the envelope I showed you. I'd like to know what's on it. Maybe he still has it on him."

When I reached out to check Wang's pockets, Irene pushed me away.

"Do not touch him!"

"Ms. Chow. That recording might tell us who killed your son. You want to know. Don't you?"

"All right. You want something Joe has? Take it."

"Maybe it's in one of his pockets," I said, checking the pockets of his pants. "Yeah. Here's what I wanted." I pulled out the MP3 player with the ear buds still attached.

"Five years I waited," Irene moaned. "Now he is dead."

Putting the earbuds in my ears, I pushed the play button and listened.

"What does it say?" Chow asked.

I removed the earbuds. "Joe was wrong."

"Wrong about what?"

"Michelle Bai, the woman who told me her name was Nikki Kwan. He thought she had tipped the police about his gambling operations and got him sent to prison."

"Well, didn't she?"

"No."

"Then, who was it? Tell me, Mr. Bishop."

"Jimmy Cho."

A hand flew to Irene's mouth. "We trusted him. Jimmy Cho told the police about my son?" She broke down again, sobbing, "Joe... Oh, Joe."

I put a hand on her shoulder. "What do you mean, you trusted him? Wasn't Cho your son's competitor?"

After several moments, Irene regained a semblance of her composure.

"Not competitors. They were in similar businesses, but Jimmy Cho and my son were on friendly terms. Cho came to me with a proposition after they put Joe in prison."

"What kind of proposition?"

"He offered to reopen China Doll and to restart the lottery for a percentage of the profits and to operate it for Joe until he got out of prison. I visited Joe at the prison and told him about the offer. Joe agreed and told me to give the money I was holding for him to Jimmy Cho to buy China Doll back from the county at the auction. Cho paid me Joe's share for five years and had agreed to turn the operation back over to my son when he got out of jail."

"Maybe Cho changed his mind," I said. "That's if he had ever intended to keep the agreement."

"Did Jimmy Cho kill my son?"

"I don't know. All the recording proves is he got Joe arrested and sent to prison. The cops will have to find out who killed Joe. I need to call them."

"No! I don't trust the cops. I want to hire you to find out who killed my son."

"Ms. Chow, I'm a private investigator, not an assassin."

"I'm not asking you to kill anyone. I will pay you one thousand dollars to find out who killed my son. If you succeed, you need only to give me the name and I will pay you another one thousand dollars."

The smart thing would have been to turn her down flat. As a private investigator, I could lose my license for working on something that would soon be an active police investigation. But two thousand dollars would go a long way toward solving my current financial difficulties.

"Will you do it, Mr. Bishop? Will you help me find out who killed my son?"

"I'll try, Ms. Chow."

"All right. Come to the Blue Goose this evening. I'll give you the first thousand."

"Okay."

She took her son's head in her hands, and whispered and crooned to him the way she must have done when he was two years old. I stood, turned, and tiptoed out of the apartment to give her some privacy. The jig-saw puzzle that had started when a frightened young woman had phoned my office was shaping into a picture. It wasn't a pretty one. But I still wondered about a couple of missing pieces. I took out my phone and called Lieutenant David Chang.

Chapter Twenty-One

Sergeant Rowden answered the phone. I asked for David.

"Oh, it's you Bishop. What do you want from the police department now?"

"I want the police department to get rid of its stupidest sergeant. A guy named Rowden."

"Ha-ha. You're not funny, Bishop. Hang on."

A moment later, David came on the line.

"Now look, Rick, if you have another corpse, take it to another police station."

"I can't do that, David. It's in Chinatown, your district."

"Nuts. Oh, all right. Who is it this time?"

"Joe Wang."

"Joe Wang? What did you kill him for?"

"I didn't kill him, David. His mother, Irene Chow, found him shot to death inside his apartment. I only came here to talk to Wang."

"The apartment at the address you gave me Saturday?"

"That's the one."

"Okay, I'll have Rowden call the coroner and the crime lab. Then we'll be along after I have some Alka-Seltzer."

David hung up.

I went back inside to tell Irene the police were on the way. I asked if she wanted me to wait with her.

"No, I want to be alone with my son."

"Okay, Ms. Chow. I'll see you later at the club."

She nodded, and I left. David had sounded like he was in a bad mood, so I was happy to leave before he arrived with his blockhead sergeant.

What I wanted to do was to forget Joe Wang and the entire mess, rent a scooter, and ride out to Lanikai Beach to take a swim and then lie on the sand and soak up some sun. But the beautiful mirage of that two grand sure looked inviting. So, instead, I wore out a little more shoe leather walking to China Doll on North Hotel Street to pay a visit to Jimmy Cho.

China Doll explicitly embraced a Chinese style. A rarity within Honolulu's Chinatown, its dramatic, neon lit, pagoda-like tower frequently stood as a touchstone image of the district. The tiled roof and fretted transom windows of the building augmented its heritage statement. A second tower, part of a rooftop pavilion, expanded to form an enclosed third floor. China Doll, principally a nightclub, didn't get the crowds until after six in the evening. But by day, it masqueraded as a bar, so it was open for business when I walked in at eleven in the morning.

I walked directly to the bar and told the bartender I wanted to see Jimmy Cho. He gave me a dubious look, but picked up the phone and made a call. A few moments later, a big guy in a suit with a bulge under his arm came down the stairs into the bar. The bartender made eye contact with him and then nodded his head toward me. I assumed he must be Cho's receptionist, but he did his best to be as unreceptive as possible.

"So, you wish to see Mr. Cho? Do you have an appointment?"

"No, I don't have an appointment. Now tell Cho I'm out here."

"What's your name?"

"It will be a mouthful for you. The name is Huckleberry Winterkorn."

"What?"

"Now, see? No need to strain your brain cells. You don't look like you have many to spare. Just make like an office boy and go tell Cho that Huckleberry Winterkorn wants to have a word with him."

"You're a funny man, aren't you?"

"Yeah, but you won't find it so funny if I have to stand around here much longer."

"You may stand here all day for all I care," the man blustered, pulling himself up to his full and considerable height. "You cannot see Mr. Cho. He is busy."

"Okay, if you don't stop getting so excited, you're going to have stomach problems someday."

"I do not think so."

"You don't, huh?" I said, as I buried my right fist into his stomach twice in rapid succession. Then I followed it up with a left and right combination that sent him reeling backward against the bar. I walked over, took his feet out from under him with a foot sweep, and then kicked him in the head to put him to sleep.

"Skeptic," I said, as I reached inside his jacket and pulled the semi-automatic out of his shoulder holster. I dumped the magazine, cleared the chamber, and then field stripped the pistol. I tossed the pieces across the room and pocketed the magazine.

When I looked at the bartender, his eyes were wide and his Adam's apple bobbed up and down.

"Can you direct me to Cho's office, pal?"

The bartender pointed a shaky finger at the stairs. "First door on the right, at the head of the stairs," he stammered.

I took the stairs two at a time, opened the first door on the right, and then crossed the small reception area to another door. I opened it too, without knocking, and walked into the private office. Jimmy Cho, seated behind a desk, looked up at me in surprise.

"Mr. Bishop? What are you doing here?"

"Collecting scalps."

"Good for you. How did you get by Chen?"

"He's got a stomach ache. He swallowed a fist, so he's taking a nap."

"All right. So, you're a tough guy. What do you want?"

"A guy named Mageo tried to kill me the other day, and I think you were behind it. I don't like getting pushed around."

"I don't know what you're talking about, Bishop. Never heard of the guy."

"I don't think you understand, Jimmy. I'm pretty mad. And I've got some questions about the murders of Joe Wang and Michelle Bai, and I'm going to get some answers, even if I have to be unpleasant with you."

"Just what do you mean by unpleasant, Mr. Bishop?"

"You get a broken arm. That's unpleasant..."

I stopped talking when I saw Cho reaching into his desk drawer. Putting both hands on the front of the desk and, using my legs, I drove the desk back, pinning Cho and his chair against the wall and pinning his hand in the drawer that had just slammed shut. Cho shrieked in pain.

"Don't try to pull a gun on me. It only makes me angrier."

"You broke my hand," he bellowed. "Take your weight off the desk and let me get my hand out."

"Let go of the gun, and I'll let you remove your hand."

"My hand is broken," he moaned.

I eased my weight off the front of the desk.

"Now take your hand out, empty."

Cho removed his injured right hand from the drawer and cradled it against his chest in his left, groaning, but visibly relieved to have his right hand out of the desk drawer. I shoved the desk hard again to shut the drawer.

"Let's start again. Why did you hire Mageo to kill Chong Pong to frame me and then to try to kill me?"

"I told you I don't know the man."

I punched Cho in the face, breaking his nose. He moaned again, unsure whether to continue cradling his broken right hand or use his left hand to hold his nose to staunch the bleeding.

"Cho, please believe me. I can keep this up all day and into the evening. Better stop lying to me."

"I told you, I don't..."

I slapped him hard with an open right hand. He cried out.

"Okay, we'll come back to that. Tell me about Joe Wang and Michelle Bai. Did you kill them or have them killed?"

"I don't know anything about..."

I slapped him hard again, making him howl.

"Listen, Bishop. I've got guys that will take care of you."

"Who's going to tell them to do it?"

"I am," he bellowed.

"With your broken jaw wired shut?" I said, hitting him with a right cross.

"Oof."

"I don't think I'm getting through to you, Cho."

"I know nothing about any murders," he whimpered. "What do you want me to do?"

"I want you to go to sleep," I said, punching him in the mouth with a straight right.

Cho's head snapped back, and then his head lolled forward with his chin on his chest. He was out cold.

I shook the sting out of my right hand and called it a day. I left the office, took the stairs back down, and walked out the front door.

Cho had told me nothing. I hadn't expected him to. I was only stirring the pot. When you didn't have the answers to something, sometimes all you could do was shake the palm tree and see if anything fell out besides coconuts. I walked back toward my office, stopping for lunch on the way. Since I'd just shaken the tree, I should have been ready for what happened next when something fell out. The only excuse I'll offer for not being ready is my mind is never as sharp on a full stomach when all I can think about is taking a nap.

Chapter Twenty-Two

I HAD JUST WRUNG out and hung the last of my washed socks and underwear, and was sitting at my desk shooting bent paperclips with a rubber band at a horsefly on the wall when my door opened. A wiry, weasel looking guy in a gray suit walked in.

"You Richard Bishop, the private detective?"

"Yes. I've stopped denying it. If you want to hire me, take out a fat wallet or checkbook and have a seat."

I got my first inkling the guy wasn't a prospective client with a cheating wife when, instead of a wallet, he pulled a large semi-automatic from inside his jacket. My second clue was the massive fellow who blocked out the sun as he ducked his head to enter the still open doorway. The skin on my neck tried to crawl down my back.

"Are you guys together?" I asked the enormous man.

"Yes, this is Tiny," the thin man said. "Tiny doesn't talk much except with his fists."

Tiny's arms looked like hairy tree trunks with twelve-pound hams on the ends of them.

"Show me your hands, and then get up and walk around to the front of the desk," the smaller guy said, waving the gun for emphasis before pointing it back at my chest.

Caught with my proverbial pants down, I had no options. I dropped the rubber band and complied.

"Didn't your mother ever teach you it isn't polite to point?" I asked the skinny guy.

"Ha-ha," he replied. "You can stop with the comedy. We're not here for laughs."

He stepped to my right and walked closer, still pointing the gun at me. Tiny walked up and stood in front of me, looking down at me with a bored expression.

"Two things, Bishop," the thin man said. "Keep your nose in your own business and stay away from Jimmy Cho and his club."

"I can do that."

"Well, we got paid to make sure that you do. We can't just take your word for it. Go ahead, Tiny."

Tiny slammed his fists together. Unfortunately, my head was between them. Then he used my face for a speed bag for a while, before driving a ham into my stomach a few times. Each time, it felt like his enormous fist rebounded off my spine. I'm not much of a fighter in the afternoons, not that I or anyone else would have been a match for Tiny without a shoulder-mounted anti-tank weapon. So, I went down faster than a base runner with a leg cramp. The floor gave way and I dropped into that black hole that seems to always show up when somebody puts me to sleep the hard way. I just kept falling like a pebble down a mine shaft, down into a whirlpool of sickly, swirling colors until I landed with a splat and the colors swallowed me up. I didn't even feel Tiny stomping and kicking me. Well, not until much later anyway.

It's easy to relax after a good beating. You just lay on the floor, bleed a little, and grow weak. From somewhere far away, I heard a voice calling my name and vaguely felt somebody slapping my face. When someone tries to shake you out of unconsciousness, it's like an alcoholic who got smashed on mouthwash. It's hard to make sense of anything.

"Come on, Rick. Let's go. Snap out of it."

"Mm... Mm... What? Oh..."

"Come on, Rick. You're a mess."

"What? Hm... Oh, yeah. Okay. We have a party or something?"

"Sort of looks that way. Come on now, wake up."

Forcing my eyelids apart, I looked up and saw David Chang's face come into focus.

"Oh my. What happened?"

"Try to sit up," David said, pulling on my jacket to help me. "The ambulance will be here in a minute. Someone beat the stuffing out of you. Where do you hurt?"

"Everywhere," I groaned. "Why didn't you let me sleep?"

"I wanted to know if you were dead. I had to try bringing you around to find out if we needed an ambulance or the coroner."

Probing my mouth with the tip of my tongue, I felt several loose teeth. But at least I still had all thirty-two. Tiny had knocked none of them out, bless his tiny heart.

"Who did this to you, Rick?"

"A gorilla named Tiny. I didn't catch his last name. Just his fists."

I heard Rowden call out from somewhere in the room. "The paramedics are coming up the stairs, Lieutenant."

"All right, Rowden. Now shut up."

"Rick, you take it easy. They'll check you out and we'll get you to the hospital. When you're well enough, you can come down and look at mugshots and we'll get the guys who did this."

The paramedics came in. The two guys prodded and probed me for a while and pronounced me concussed. They said I might have a skull fracture, a fractured jaw, some broken ribs, and that I needed stitches above both eyes. They put a neck collar on me and then helped me downstairs to the ambulance. David rode in the back with me on the way to the hospital and Rowden followed in their car.

"How did you find me?"

"I wanted to get your statement about the Wang killing since you took off before we got to his apartment. When you didn't answer your phone, I decided to stop by your office to see if you were there. We found the door open."

At The Queens Medical Center, an ER doctor looked me over. Then they took my clothes off, put me in a hospital gown, and rolled me down for X-rays. After that, they gave me an MRI. Then, they put me in a room. David and Rowden were there waiting.

"Please, David, can't Rowden wait in the hall? Haven't I been through enough without having to look at him?"

"Very funny, gumshoe. But not nearly as funny as your face looks."

"Rowden?" David said.

"Yes, Lieutenant?"

"Shut up and get out of here."

"Oh, okay, Lieutenant," Rowden said, looking chastened. "But he started it." Then he left the room.

A gray-haired doctor came in carrying a chart.

"How are you feeling, Mr. Bishop?" he said.

"Okay, doc. Just a little sore."

"That's no surprise, young man. You look like Rocky Balboa after ten rounds with Apollo Creed."

"Just cut me, doc, so I can see. No way you're stopping this fight."

The doctor chuckled. I don't think we need to do that. But I need to stitch up those cuts over your eyes.

"How is he, doctor?" David asked.

"He should make a full recovery," the doctor said to David, before turning to me.

"Mr. Bishop, you have a concussion, but no skull fracture. Your head should be all right in time unless you develop a brain bleed. You have only a hairline jaw fracture, so we don't need to wire it shut. And you have three cracked ribs and some minor internal injuries, so expect some blood in your urine for a while. Overall, you have the injuries we often see in a patient who has been in a severe car crash. We're keeping you here for observation. Pending any complications from the concussion, we will probably send you home in a few days. Questions?"

"I think you covered all the bases, doc."

"Fine, I have to check on another patient. Then I'll be back to stitch up those lacerations."

After the doctor left the room, I looked at David.

"Did they bring my clothes in here?"

"Yes, they put them in the closet over there. Why?"

"Get me my pants," I said. "I've got to get out of here."

"You're not going anywhere, Rick. I'm not letting you go after those guys alone for beating you up. I won't have it. Let us handle it after you've looked at mugshots and identified them. Guys like that are bound to have records."

"Believe me, I have no intention of having a rematch with Tiny. I have no medical insurance and a collection agency is already hot on my heels for the bill I ran up the last time I was here. I can't afford any more medical expenses. Now get me my pants."

Grumbling, David retrieved my clothes from the closet while I sat on the edge of the bed, recovering from a dizzy spell.

"I don't like this crazy idea," David mumbled while I got dressed.

"I can't waste the time or the money staying in a hospital, David. I've got places to go and people to see. And by recuperating at Sally's place, I'll avoid more medical bills I can't afford to pay."

"Okay, but when we get out of here, I'm driving you straight to Sally's house."

David called Rowden back into the room. They helped me to the door, and when the coast was clear, they helped me down the hall to the stairwell to avoid the nurses' station. We made it out of the hospital and out to the unmarked car Rowden had parked in a space for emergency vehicles.

In the backseat of the car, I pulled out my phone, called the Blue Goose, and asked for Irene Chow. No one had ever beaten me badly enough to make me forget that someone had promised me money. And after the beating I'd just suffered, I felt I'd already earned Irene Chow's first thousand. When she came on the line, I told her I was on the way to collect the retainer. Then I told her I'd been in an accident and had difficulty walking. I asked if I called back when I arrived if she would send someone out to my car with the money. She agreed, and we hung up.

"David, I need to make a quick stop before you drive me to Sally's condo."

"I don't think that's a good idea, Rick."

"Come on, David. It will only take a minute and I won't even get out of the car."

"Oh, all right. Where are we going?"

"Chinatown. The Blue Goose Club."

Chapter Twenty-Three

ROWDEN SPED THROUGH THE night and ten minutes later pulled up in front of the Blue Goose. I phoned Irene again, told her I was outside, and described the unmarked police car. A few minutes later, the front door opened and Irene herself came out with an envelope in her hand. I had Rowden lower my window as she approached. Irene looked at me with shock and then glanced at Rowden and David.

"What happened to you?" she asked. "You get hit by a pineapple truck?"

"I fell down some stairs?"

"Fell down some stairs? You look like you fell out of an airplane."

"It was a lot of stairs. I was messing around on the upper deck at Aloha Stadium and fell down the stairs all the way to field level."

Irene looked unconvinced, then she glanced again with suspicion at the two cops.

"Who are these gentlemen?"

"My bowling league partners. We've got a tournament tonight."

"I thought you said you could barely walk, and looking at you, I believe that much."

"Oh, I'll be fine. I'll just have to adjust my approach a little. Anyway, don't worry. You can talk in front of these guys. They know how to keep their mouths shut."

"All right. Have you learned anything yet about what we discussed?"

"Yes, I started the job today, and already know a lot more now than I did when we talked earlier."

"Like what?"

"I learned Jimmy Cho is hiding something. I just don't know if he is the guy yet. So, I need to make further inquiries."

"You sure you're well enough to do the job?"

"Oh, sure. By tomorrow, I'm sure I'll be good as new. I've always been a fast healer."

"Well, all right." Irene said, passing me the envelope through the window. "Call me when you find out... you know... what I asked you to find out."

"Count on it."

Irene nodded, then turned and walked back towards the club's entrance.

"What was that all about?" David asked as Rowden raised my window and drove out of the parking lot.

"I'm doing a minor job for Irene Chow. Nothing that would interest you, David."

David grumbled something, but asked no more questions. He turned his head and stared out the windshield.

Another ten minutes later, Rowden stopped in front of Sally's condo building. They helped me inside and into the elevator and we said goodnight. I rode the elevator up to Sally's floor.

I rang the bell and a few moments later, Cooper opened the door.

"Yes?"

"You don't have a stretcher handy, do you, Cooper?"

"Oh, my goodness, Mr. Bishop. I didn't recognize you, sir."

"In the flesh. Mangled flesh though it is."

"Oh, come in, sir. Come in."

"Thank you, Cooper."

I shambled inside and Cooper closed the door.

"Shall I get you some steaks for those eyes, sir?"

"No, thanks. Just run along and tell Ms. Fisher that sweet and bloody is here."

Sally called from the lounge.

"Who is it, Cooper?"

She appeared in the doorway and looked at me.

"Oh, no!" she shrieked, a hand flying to her mouth. "Is that you, Ricky?"

"That's a good question. If it's not me, what are you doing with a strange man in your house? You know how jealous I am."

"Cooper!"

"Yes, Ms. Fisher. Ice bags and the first aid kit you bought last time."

"Good old Florence Nightingale in a houseboy's uniform," I said.

"Stop the wisecracks and come through to the lounge," Sally said.

"Yes, ma'am." I shuffled into the living room with my arm over Sally's shoulders and her arm around my waist.

"Now sit down."

"Yes ma'am."

"Why aren't you in a hospital?"

"I was. They wrapped my cracked ribs, and then I discharged myself."

"Ricky!"

She deposited me on the couch and held my face in her warm hands and inspected my injuries.

"You need stitches above both eyes. Cooper used to be a medic in the army before he came to work for us in Sydney. He can stitch you up and mummy will take care of the rest, you poor baby."

"Here you are, Ms. Fisher. Ice bags and the first aid kit."

"Just put them there on the table, Cooper. I'm going to ice the swelling and when it goes down some, I need you to suture these cuts over his eyes."

"Yes, madam. Will that be all for now?"

"Yes, thank you, Cooper. I'll call you when we're ready for the stitches."

"Yes, Ms. Fisher." Cooper bowed and left the room. Sally tilted my head back and applied the ice bags to my face.

"What on earth happened to you, Rick?"

"Oh, it's a sordid tale, full of my heroic deeds. You really wouldn't be interested."

"Rick!"

"It would take too long to tell the story. Besides, you know how modest I am. I'd feel like I was bragging."

"Oh, all right. Forget about it."

"But if you're going to insist on hearing what happened."

"No, you don't have to tell me if you don't want to."

"Well, the whole thing started four days ago when that young woman identifying herself as Nikki Kwan hired me to protect her..."

Chapter Twenty-Four

I SPENT THREE RELAXING days convalescing at Casa de Sally. The insatiable little vixen took advantage of my circumstances, ravaging me again and again as I lay feverish upon my sick bed. But the more time we spent in bed, the less time she had to talk of marriage and of us moving to Sydney, where I could work for her father to avoid being beaten up constantly. I had chided her gently, reminding her it only happened a few times a month. And I pointed out that usually somebody only sapped me or hit me on the head with a gun and that hardly qualified as a beating.

By Friday morning, I had recovered my vigor and vitality to the extent I felt fit enough to resume my investigation on Irene Chow's behalf. Sally reluctantly drove me back to Chinatown and dropped me off at my office.

I had barely finished going through my mail and adding the new bills and collection letters to the neat stacks on my desk when the door flew open and Nicole Hersey blew in like the Kona Winds. I could almost see steam emanating from her ears. She looked like Kilauea about to erupt.

"Where have you been, Richard Bishop? You've ignored my many calls and text messages and haven't been in your office in at least three days! I've checked. You've been dodging me!"

"I have done no such thing, Nicole. For your information, I fell ill on Monday, seriously ill, and have been recuperating at an undisclosed location."

Nicole's eyes locked on the blood-stained carpet. "What happened here? This place looks like a charnel house."

"Well, it was more of a severe beating that felled me than an illness."

"Oh my goodness," Nicole said, her tone softening a little. "Are you all right?"

"Yes, don't worry your pretty little head about it, Nicole. Your heartfelt concern touches me deeply, but I'm well on the road to recovery."

"Good," she said, the fire returning to her eyes. "I'd hate for anything serious to happen to you until you've paid this."

Nicole slapped a paper on my desk. I picked it up and read the itemized list. One queen-size mattress and box springs, a set of Egyptian cotton sheets, and a quilted comforter.

"What's this?" I demanded, waving the paper at her.

"An invoice for what I spent to clean up your mess, Richard. Someone bled out and died in my guestroom. Remember?"

"Nicole, surely you don't hold me responsible for that. Besides, I only saw a little blood on the top sheet and comforter. You didn't need to replace the entire bed."

"You're lucky I salvaged the headboard and frame. I'm not asking a future house guest to sleep in a murder bed? If you don't have cash, I'll risk accepting your personal check."

"Look, Nicole. You're the one who made the poor decision to take a stranger into your home you knew nothing about. I cannot see why you're trying to hold me responsible for your mistake."

"My mistake!" she shrieked. "You pressured me into letting that woman stay with me and didn't bother warning me someone might break into my house and stab her to death. Richard, has it occurred to you that if I hadn't gone to the office that morning, I could also be dead? I doubt the murderer would have left a witness behind."

"Don't be such a drama queen, Nicole. You went to the office and were never in danger. Besides, I couldn't predict what happened. And that woman conned me. She wasn't the innocent babe in the woods she pretended to be. Nikki Kwan wasn't even her actual name. It was Michelle Bai."

Nicole stood red-faced with her hands balled into fists.

"Whatever, Richard. You're still paying for the bedding. And where is the twenty-five hundred dollars you promised me?"

"Surely you understand the murder of Michelle Bai means she never paid me the bonus for finishing the case. We're both out that money."

Nicole smiled, reached into her purse, and slapped an envelope on the desk. "Open it and weep, Richard."

"What's this?"

"I met with your auto insurer's attorney Tuesday and we settled. That's a check for you."

"What!" I exclaimed. "It's about time." Eagerly, I slit the envelope's flap with a letter opener and withdrew a check.

"What's this? Nineteen dollars and seventy-seven cents?"

"Per common practice, the insurance company made the settlement check out to the firm. We deducted my legal services fees, and that's the balance due to you."

"This is highway robbery! I'm out an almost new car and I get nineteen lousy dollars and seventy-seven stinking cents?"

"Besides the legal fees, the insurance company had to pay off your auto loan at your bank. That's the law. And I could have applied your share of the settlement to what you owe me for the bedding, but that's a personal debt. You should just be glad you no longer owe me the twenty-five hundred you promised that I'm sure you never intended to pay."

"Nicole, you wound me," I said, crossing my fingers on both hands beneath the desk. "That's hitting way below the belt. Of course, I intended to pay you the money I promised."

"Whatever. And I want the money for the bedding before I walk out of here."

I held up my open hands in a gesture of helplessness. "Nicole, I'll get it to you later. I'm broke right now. I have no dinero, not a single Bolívar. I was about to walk down to the blood bank to donate plasma just to earn enough to buy a few scraps of food for lunch."

"You know what, Richard? Just forget it. I don't want the money and I don't think we should see each other again. You're always dragging me into your drama and stiffing me for the money you owe."

"What? You're breaking up with me as a friend?"

"As a friend and I'm also dissolving our attorney-client relationship. I think we will both be better off by making a clean break of it."

"Get you," I said. "Even when you spurned my affections and broke our engagement, almost destroying my life, I never considered breaking up with you as a friend and kept bringing my legal business to you. Nicole, I've literally dug up a body for you. Doesn't that count for anything?"

"You only exhumed a casket, Richard. An empty casket. There was no corpse inside it."

"Well, yeah, if you want to split hairs, but I thought your friend's body was inside it when I dug it up. I dug it up for you in good faith."

"I wish you the best, Richard. I mean that. But our continued association will only lead me to a complete nervous breakdown."

With those parting words, Nicole Hersey turned and strode out of my life, slamming my office door behind her.

"How do you like that?" I fumed aloud, pounding my fist on my desk. I'd believed our friendship had been strong enough to weather any storm. But evidently, friends that were loyal and true were as hard to find as oranges on a coconut palm tree.

Chapter Twenty-Five

I FELT SO DEPRESSED after Nicole left that I locked up and left the office a few minutes later. I didn't even bother taking the dry laundry off the line and folding it. Then I walked down to the corner and took the bus downtown. It wasn't the loss of Nicole that bothered me so much. Attorneys were a dime a dozen. Sometimes it seemed there was a lawyer to every ten people in Hawaii. I supposed most ne'er-do-wells majored in the law until they came up with flashier degrees like international relations that also didn't qualify anyone for a paying job. Most attorneys made less money than I did, which probably explained why so many left the law and went into politics along with the international relations grads. No, I wouldn't miss Nicole. I'd have no trouble finding another lawyer if I needed one.

What really bothered me about the Nicole situation was it reminded me of how many friends I'd lost recently. Besides Nicole, there had been Gabby and Koko. Sure, I dated them both, but we had also been friends, especially Koko. Next to Joe Rose, she had once been my closest friend. The circumstances forced me to pause for some self-reflection. And I suppose I needed a word of encouragement from a friend.

I got off the bus at the stop a block from the Likelike and trudged to the club feeling blue. I opened the door and scanned the barroom before going in. Joe, sitting in his usual spot, turned to look at me. He grinned.

"Come on in, pal. The coast is clear. Koko doesn't come in until six this evening."

Relieved, I let the door close, walked to the bar, and sat on the stool beside Joe.

Moki, the bartender, put a bottle of Longboard in front of me, and then went back to stocking the beer cooler.

"Mahalo, Moki."

"No problem, Rick."

"No clients, Richard?" Joe asked.

"Actually, I have a client and I'm working on something."

"Then what are you doing here at this time of morning? Don't you still work until two most afternoons?"

"Yeah, but I took a pretty good beating Monday. I've been off the last three days recuperating. You might say I'm just easing back into the harness. That's why I left the office a little early today."

"Who beat you up this time?"

"This time? It's not like it happens every day. You sound like Sally."

"Come on, Richard. It isn't like it's an isolated occurrence. That's why I keep saying you should get your pal David Chang to get you hired back at the police department. You stay with the private detective business much longer and you're liable to end up with dementia by the time you're forty, like those fighters who take punches to the head too often."

"Joe, you don't understand how much my little private investigations agency means to me. When I wore a badge, I had too many rules to follow. I enjoy being my own boss, making enough to pay the rent and to take my girl to dinner once in a while, and putting my feet up on the desk like any other prosperous businessmen. Sure, like a lot of other working stiffs, at one o'clock in the afternoon, I get pretty eager for two o'clock to roll around. Especially if I haven't had a client in several weeks. But even if I don't expect a client to walk in before two, I don't take a chance. I stand and stare out my office window just to kill time until two. I look out on the alley behind my building and wonder just how many potential clients are out and about in the city. Who's getting in trouble, what kind of trouble, and will they come to Richard Bishop for help? That's just something I can't give up."

"Well, I only have one problem with all that?"

"Yeah? What is it?"

"That part about being like any other prosperous businessman."

"What's wrong with it?"

"Only that you aren't prosperous, Richard. You're broke all the time. At least when you were a cop, you had a steady paycheck."

"Oh, I get by, Joe. No, I'm not getting rich. But I like the work and see the job as my way of giving back to society."

"Oh, brother."

"I mean it, Joe. I wish you could be more supportive."

"All right, Richard, have it your way. You know, I'm surprised you came in here after taking off early. I haven't seen you much since you started dating the heiress. Is she at work?"

"No, I'm sure she's at home. Sally has managers that run her store. She only goes in once in a while to check in and make sure everything is running smoothly, and that the cash is still rolling in. Sally is more of an entrepreneur type than a hands-on business owner."

"Must be nice."

"I don't expect you to understand it, Joe. You're a hands-on guy. Always have been. Nothing wrong with that. That's just your management style."

"Okay, Richard. Thanks for the reassurance. I'm still wondering why you're here instead of at home with your girlfriend."

"Because we need to talk, Joe. I mean, I need to talk."

"So, talk, pal. What's on your mind?"

"Joe, do you consider me a good friend?"

"Sure, we've been pals since the Navy. I used to put my life in your hands, and you put your life in mine. You never let me down when we were in the teams. Sure, we're good friends. The best."

"That's great, Joe. But what I mean is, do you think I have qualities that make you feel it's worth having me as a friend?"

"Of course. I guess we wouldn't be friends otherwise. Richard, what's this all about. You seem... well... a little emotional today."

"Can't I have a serious conversation with my best friend?"

"Yeah, sure. But please try not to cry all over my bar. It always makes me feel so helpless."

"Joe, it just occurred to me I've lost several friends recently. Good friends. I'm just wondering if there is something wrong with me that makes people not want to stay friends with me."

"Richard, what are you talking about?"

"It's true, Joe. First Koko stopped being my friend. Then Gabby. And today, Nicole broke up with me as a friend. Is it something I'm doing, Joe? I don't understand it? Why do I keep losing friends?"

"Well, Richard, Koko and Gabby are easy enough to explain. Girls don't like it much when you're dating one and then you sleep with her best girlfriend. Or when you propose to your lawyer while you're dating some other girl."

"Joe, I explained that to you. Gabby was throwing herself at me all the time. She caught me at a weak moment and it just happened. It was an accident more than anything else."

"Sure, Richard. I understand, but some people. Not me, mind you. So, don't get mad. But some people might say you're a little selfish and only think about yourself. That you don't have enough empathy for other people and their feelings."

"Joe, that's where you're wrong. If anything, I have too much empathy for everybody I know. I hardly ever think of myself first. I think that's why I slept with Gabby. It was the empathy. And it probably explains why I proposed to Nicole. You know I'm not that interested in getting married. Just talking about it too much sends me right into a panic attack."

"Yeah, Richard. I know. You've told me all about it."

"Anyway, thanks a lot, Joe. Good talk. I guess I only needed reassurance that our friendship is still solid. I was doubting myself a little."

"Always happy to help, pal," Joe said, shaking his head.

"Oh, there was another reason I dropped by today, Joe." I took the envelope out of my inside jacket pocket and put in on the bar in front of him.

"What's this?"

"Open it, Joe."

Joe opened the envelope and looked inside.

"There's a thousand bucks in here," he said in astonishment.

"Yeah, a thousand towards what I borrowed from you."

"You only borrowed it last Sunday. Didn't you catch up on your rent?"

"Of course. But I got that for a retainer and wanted to give it to you, Joe. I'll get the rest to you in a few days."

"Yeah, sure, pal. No hurry. I was fine with waiting until your insurance settlement came in."

"No, Joe. I wanted to get the money back to you as soon as possible. As soon as I collected that thousand, I knew I wanted to bring it over."

"I guess I owe you an apology, Richard."

"For what?"

"Well, I must admit I didn't really expect to see that fifteen hundred bucks again when I gave it to you. But here you are already paying me back a thousand. I feel a little guilty for doubting you, Richard. I'm sorry about that."

"You doubted I'd pay you back, but you gave me the money anyway?"

"Well, sure. We're friends, Richard. I wouldn't refuse you a loan when I had the money. Not even if you couldn't pay me back."

"I appreciate that, Joe. It means a lot having a friend like you."

"Yeah, I'm glad to have a friend like you, Richard. You've also helped me out before. Don't think I've forgotten that."

"Yeah, whatever you need, Joe, just ask. I'm your guy."

Joe nodded and wiped his eyes.

"Hey, Joe."

"Yeah, buddy?"

"Don't cry all over your bar. It always makes me feel so helpless."

Chapter Twenty-Six

I LEFT JOE AT the club feeling much better. Yes, I'd lost a few friends recently, but I still had Joe Rose. And we were rock solid. David Chang and I were also good friends. And while I hated to admit it, I considered Rowden a friend, even though I teased him unmercifully.

With the insight I'd gained from my friend Joe, I realized maybe my problem with the friends I'd lost wasn't about just friendship at all. Maybe it was about friendships with girls. Maybe girls weren't built to be loyal and true, through thick and thin, friends. Unlike men, they operated far more on emotions than logic. And I had no problems with my guy friendships.

Don't get me wrong. Women have their redeeming qualities. No one appreciated that more than I did. But maybe, when push came to shove, you just couldn't count on them for friendship. I felt a little foolish just realizing that truth. After all, no one I'd ever met understood women better than I did.

The talk with Joe also reminded me of why I enjoyed my job as a private investigator. Sure, I was in business because I liked money. And why not? Keeping yourself fed, a roof over your head, and having the ability to pay bills when you had a little extra all required money. Even a guy who loved his work as much as I did couldn't afford to work for free.

Of course, I could do better, but I didn't believe in exerting myself more than necessary. Yes, I could find work where I could make a few more bucks by working harder. But so what? People worked harder to make more money only to grow weaker, mentally or physically. Then they spent all that extra money on therapists or doctor bills. No, I had my little second-floor walk up office on Hotel Street and I was very happy. I got by just fine as long as I had a few clients at three hundred a day, plus expenses each month. And I had a partner called human nature to help. Having human nature on my side meant people were naturally going to get in trouble. And when trouble came around, people came to me for help. That's how a private investigator makes his living.

It occurred to me I had wanted to go for a swim out at Lanikai Beach since Monday morning. That was just the ticket to help me relax so I could focus on planning my next move in the search for Joe Wang's killer. I headed towards Coconut Willy's Scooter Rentals on Uluniu Avenue. I could catch a bus out to Lanikai Beach, but a scooter was faster. And I'd have no trouble getting back in time for dinner at Sally's condo. She expected me at seven o'clock.

Unlike guys with something to compensate for, I didn't need a big Harley between my legs to enjoy the open road and the wind on my face. Just give me a sporty 50cc scooter and I was happy as a clam. For one thing, scooters were more economical on gas, which was prohibitively expensive in Hawaii, especially since Biden got elected.

I'd turned the corner and got halfway up Uluniu when a black sedan pulled up beside me and stopped at the curb. My old friend Tiny threw open the door, unfolded himself like an accordion from the front passenger seat, and grabbed me by the collar. He moved fast for such a big guy. Through the open car door, I saw his pal, the weasel, sitting behind the wheel.

"Not you guys again," I said. "Listen, Tiny. Don't you know the surgeon general warns that getting beaten half to death more than once a year is hazardous to your health?"

"Cut out the funny business, Bishop," the weasel shouted out the open door. "Get in the car before I have Tiny break something."

I'd left the office in such a hurry that I'd forgotten to bring my gun with me. It was still in my desk drawer. And without it, it was useless to argue. Tiny opened the rear passenger door and threw me into the backseat. Then he closed the front passenger door and climbed in the back with me. Being in the backseat with him felt like being in a can of sardines with all their relatives visiting. I felt my claustrophobia kicking up. The weasel pulled away from the curb and continued down Uluniu.

"They must have made you of rubber, Bishop," he said over his shoulder. "I figured Tiny bounced you hard enough to put you in a hospital for at least a week. But you're already walking around, causing trouble. I guess you didn't take us seriously."

"What do you mean? I've followed our agreement religiously."

"Only half of it, shamus. You must have forgotten the part about minding your own business. Someone told the boss you're working for Irene Chow, looking for her son's killer. We know you collected a retainer from her Monday night after we talked last time."

The weasel made a left onto Kuhio.

"Where are we going?" I asked.

"We're going to a nice hotel room to hang out until dark," the weasel said. "Then when it's good and dark, we're going to take a drive out to Halona Blowhole."

"If you've got Eternity Beach in mind, I don't swim there after dark. The waves and currents at night are too unpredictable."

"You won't be swimming. Just diving."

The weasel stopped for the light at Kaiulani Avenue beside the bus stop. A bus was there loading passengers and about to drive away. The only thing I liked less than swimming at Eternity Beach after dark was the idea of cliff diving at Halona Blowhole, day or night. So, I had to make a move fast. I lifted my bent legs, spun my butt on the seat to the right, and braced my back against the car door. Then, like a government mule, I kicked Tiny in the head with both hooves. His head ricocheted off the glass of the car door on his side. I hadn't got enough into it to put Tiny to sleep, but I stunned him long enough to open the door on my side and bail out.

It had all happened so fast that the weasel hadn't had time to react to my jail break. I hot-footed it around the back of the car and then the bus, squeezing through the front door just as the driver closed it. I showed him my bus pass. The bus lurched ahead, and I looked out a window to see the weasel and Tiny standing on the sidewalk watching. I guess they didn't like seeing me go. They didn't wave goodbye.

Knowing the two hoods would overtake the bus with the car in short order and that Tiny would then board and drag me off the bus, I jumped off at the next stop and ducked into a coffee shop. I walked straight through to the back, went through a door into the back room, and then out the rear service entrance into the alley. In the alley, I made like a track star and hoofed it back toward Uluniu.

Cutting through an apartment complex, I arrived back at Kuhio and jogged to a bus stop beside a hotel. Five minutes later, I boarded a number 13 bus and rode towards Chinatown. I was on my way to see Lieutenant Chang at the police station on South Beretania Street. It was time to identify Tiny and his pal so the cops could take them out of circulation.

After a twenty-minute ride, I got off the bus at the Alapai and South King Street stop. Then I made the three-minute walk to the police station.

Sergeant Rowden looked up when I walked into the squad room.

"Oh, it's you, Bishop. What do you want?"

"I want to borrow one of your shoes, Rowden. I want to take my girl sailing this weekend."

"Hey, funny guy, you're not funny. You better go on in and see the lieutenant. I'm too busy to waste time listening to your stupid jokes."

"Busy doing what?"

"I've got to finish these reports for the lieutenant."

"Look at you, Rowden. You finally figured it out. The department hired you to work."

I opened the door and went into David's office without waiting for Rowden's repartee, knowing he had nothing. In a battle of wits, Rowden was unarmed.

"Hello, David."

"Rick, I've been looking all over town for you. Why don't you ever answer your phone?"

"Why don't you cops get on the job? It's getting where it isn't safe for a citizen to walk the streets of Honolulu at high noon."

"What are you yapping about?"

"I leave Joe's club to walk to Coconut Willy's Scooter Rentals to rent a ride for the afternoon, and those two goons from Monday night try to abduct me in broad daylight."

"That's your own fault, Rick. You haven't bothered to come in to identify them so we can pick them up. Lucky you got away from them this time."

"Okay, I'm here now and ready to look at pictures. I want those two out of circulation."

"All right. I've already pulled booking photos for everyone in the system from the alias database with the nickname Tiny. Take a look and see if you recognize the guy that gave you the beating."

I walked behind David's desk so I could see his computer screen.

"No, it's none of them."

David clicked the mouse, and another group of photos popped onto the screen. I scanned them from left to right, row by row.

"There," I said, tapping the screen with my finger. "That's the guy."

"Yeah, that's Lani 'Tiny' Aiulu. He's one rough boy. You're lucky he didn't kill you the first time you ran into him. Okay, let me search for his known associates."

David typed on the keyboard and in a moment, a new smaller group of photos came up on the screen. Fewer photos to choose from made it easier to spot the weasel guy.

"There, that's him. The skinny guy with the big gun. He was driving the car today when they accosted me on Uluniu."

"Okay, that's Robert Lukela. What kind of car?"

"Tiny hustled me into a black Honda Accord sedan. I shoved my feet into his face, bailed out, and beat it onto a bus. So, I was too busy running for my life to get the license plate number."

David picked up the phone and dialed.

"Rowden, I want arrest warrants for Lani Aiulu and Robert Lukela. The charges are kidnapping and aggravated assault. And put out an APB to all units to arrest and detain those two for questioning if located. They are driving a black Honda Accord sedan, with an unknown license plate number."

"I can narrow it down for you a little, David. Tiny busted the right back passenger door glass, hitting it with his head on the rebound."

David passed the tidbit on to Rowden and hung up the phone.

"Well, even without the license plate number, with every cop in the city looking for them and the car, I think we'll get them pretty fast."

"You know who they work for?"

"Yeah, Jimmy Cho."

"Wow. That explains something."

"What?"

"I can't prove it yet, but I think Jimmy Cho might have killed Joe Wang, or had him killed. Monday morning, after I left Wang's apartment, I went to China Doll and had a talk with Jimmy. I got a little rough with him while trying to find out if he was good for the murder."

"Did he admit anything?"

"No. Jimmy got tired of talking and took a nap, so I left."

"Then he sent Aiulu and Lukela to your office when he woke up to repay the favor."

"Sounds about right. Aiulu did the beating, and Lukela did all the talking. He told me to keep my nose in my own business and to stay away from Jimmy Cho and China Doll."

"So, you kicked over a hornet's nest."

"Yeah, and Aiulu and Lukela flew out. I hadn't expected Cho to confess to anything. I was only shaking the old palm tree to see what fell out. Only I wasn't ready for it when the coconuts started smacking me on the head."

"Is that what Irene Chow hired you to do? To find out who killed her son?"

"David, you know I can't tell you that. My clients expect me to protect their privacy. If word got out that I spilled my guts to the cops about my cases, I'd be out of business."

"Now you listen to me, Rick. You know you can't interfere in an active police investigation. If the chief finds out you're nosing around in the Wang murder, he'll pull your license and Rowden will be running the criminal investigation division if he finds out I knew about it and didn't stop you."

"Then he better not find out, David. I'm only trying to help you catch a killer."

"Oh, you idiot," David said, picking up the phone.

"Rowden, you get those warrants working and the APB put out? Okay, fine. Then bring me a glass of water for my Alka-Seltzer."

David slammed the phone down.

"David, you drink enough of that stuff to neutralize Kilauea."

"You shut up," David said, pointing his finger at me. "It's all your fault that I have a sour stomach all the time."

Rowden opened the door and came in.

"Here you go, Lieutenant. I put the Alka-Seltzer in your top, right-hand drawer."

"Thanks, now get out of here, pineapple head."

"Geez, what did I do?" Rowden asked. He opened the door and went out, shaking his head.

My cell phone rang. I took it out, answered, and got the worst news I'd had in a long while.

Chapter Twenty-Seven

IT WAS COOPER ON the phone, calling from Sally's condominium. He sounded frantic and a little woozy.

"Oh, Mr. Bishop, thank goodness. Please hurry over here. Something has happened to Ms. Fisher."

"What are you talking about?"

"Two men kidnapped Ms. Fisher."

"What?"

"Yes, sir. An enormous fellow and a thin, smaller gentleman. They took Ms. Fisher from the house at gunpoint. When they rang the doorbell, the large fellow struck me on the head the moment I opened the door. I think I must have blacked out for a moment. By the time I got downstairs in the lift and to the entrance, they were putting Ms. Fisher in a black sedan, and then they drove away. Oh, my goodness. It was terrible, and I'm afraid I was quite useless."

"Don't beat yourself up, Cooper. I think I know who the men were and believe me, there was nothing you could have done to stop them. Just wait there. I'll be right over with Lieutenant Chang."

"Yes, sir."

"We have to get over to Sally's place, David. Someone kidnapped her."

"Someone kidnapped her?"

"Yeah, they pulled a gun on her and slugged Cooper. From his descriptions of the men, I'll give you eight to five odds that it was Aiulu and Lukela. Print their mugshots so we can take them with us. I want to show them to Cooper to make sure it was them."

"Why would they kidnap Sally?"

"Because I gave them the slip earlier. Using Sally is a sure way to get me to come out to play, saving them the trouble of finding me again."

"Don't worry, Rick. We will find her."

"Hey, David, can you print me a second set of those photos?"

"Sure, but what are you going to do?"

"See if I can find the kidnappers. You go on over and talk to Cooper. See if these are the same guys who took Sally. I'm going down to a bar on Kalani Street to talk to a wise old bird who knows about things like this."

I got out of the police station in a hurry and grabbed a cab for Kalani Street. With Sally at the mercy of two hoodlums, I wasn't about to pinch pennies riding the bus. I had recently become reacquainted with an old alcoholic from my police days who had a line on every crook in Chinatown and there was just a chance she could tell me where Aiulu and Lukela were hiding out with Sally. I suspected it might be the same hotel room they had planned to take me before I had escaped.

I entered the shabby dive called the Harbor Lounge, the favorite watering hole of Glenda Mills. I found the old bird perched on the same stool she had been sitting on the first time I'd met her at the bar.

"Hello, Glenda."

"What? Well, well. The prodigal copper has returned. I would rise and curtsy as befits the occasion, but fear my rheumatism forces me to remain in a sitting position."

"I haven't the time for small talk, Glenda. I'm looking for someone. Here."

I handed her the two booking photos.

"Take a look at those pictures. You ever see those guys?"

"Unless I've had my afternoon libation, Detective, I can bring nothing into focus but a large gin bottle."

"Ah, okay. Oh, bartender! Bartender, give me a bottle of what my friend here is drinking."

"You have arrived in the nick of time. I get that wonderful warm glow when you ask for a whole bottle. Of course, it might be hot flashes. I get those too from time to time."

"Yeah, okay, Glenda. Now, tell me. Do you know these men?"

"One glass from this fifth of strength, and I will have the eyes of a Pueo, the Hawaiian short-eared owl."

I filled Glenda's empty glass with gin. She poured it down her throat without a pause. She picked up the photos from the bar.

"Now... yes, I can see these gentlemen clearly. In fact, my vision has so greatly improved. I see them in such great detail I can readily see from his squinty eyes and prominent brow that this one here is a person of doubtful character."

"But do you know them?"

"This one with the thin face is Mr. Robert Lukela, and the other is his associate, Mr. Lani Aiulu. Some call him by the nickname Tiny. Though I assure you that the moniker refers to his mental capacity, not his stature. I believe he is about six-foot-eight and weighs close to four hundred pounds."

"You're batting a thousand so far, Glenda. Do you know where I can find them?"

"Until recently, they resided in a state institution. Halawa Correctional Facility, I believe. Now, it's very possible they are staying at one of their old haunts on Kalakaua Avenue. But I couldn't say for sure."

"Ah? Why not?"

"This bottle you purchased entitles you to one of my best guesses. Further inducement would be necessary if you wish absolute accuracy."

Glenda glanced around the bar, and then whispered, "It's the risk involved in telling you where to find them, Detective."

I nodded and flagged the bartender again. "Bring me another bottle, bartender."

"Ah, bless you. Try looking at a... shall we say, reasonably priced, economy hotel called the Moanalua on the eastern end of Waikiki near Diamond Head. Sadly, I don't know the room number."

"That's okay. Glenda. I think I can figure that part out."

"Wonderful. In that case, I won't detain you here in a lengthy conversation. I'm sure you're busy and I'll need all my concentration for the work ahead of me. Goodbye, Detective, and please stop in again. Tomorrow perhaps, if you wake feeling charitable."

I left Glenda trying to figure out the best way to handle the two bottles and headed in the taxi for the address she had given me, feeling sure the information was worth what I'd paid for the cheap gin. I'd read about the Moanalua Hotel in the paper recently.

The hotel, now named the Moanalua, had been a stylish and popular hotel in its day but had long since fallen into decline with its advanced age. A development company had purchased the property with the intentions of razing it and building luxurious condominiums in its place. But the federal government had joined a Native Hawaiian activist group in a lawsuit filed that had blocked the planned development.

The activist group's vision was to use the site to build more affordable housing for Native Hawaiians. While the last few decades had seen only a slight increase in the Native Hawaiian population, it seemed new activist groups sprung up near daily marching to the drumbeat of claims that the Native Hawaiian community bore a burden of the lack of affordable housing that was disparate. The affordable housing crisis, they claimed, served as an existential threat to Hawaiian culture and that it was time to acknowledge that Native Hawaiians owned a special right to housing.

Mostly the issue behind the lawsuit and the entire affordable housing activist movement stemmed from the longstanding resentment toward the loss of Hawaiian sovereignty and how Hawaii became the fiftieth state. Many Native Hawaiians wanted a Native Hawaiians' first policy and all property to be used to benefit Native Hawaiians, not for the benefit of the haole tourists who flocked there or the mainland corporations that owned or controlled great swaths of property in Hawaii.

While the future of the Moanalua property remained mired in the courts, the development company continued to operate the hotel under its current name as a low-budget offering and spent little more than the minimum required to keep it open. So, the hotel was popular with those who were perhaps only a step or two from homelessness. That's one reason I expected to find Lukela and Aiulu living there. Also, Lukela had promised me a late-night drive to Halona Blowhole, on HI-72, about twelve miles from Waikiki, after spending the day in a hotel room. The hotel's location offered easy access to HI-72, so the Moanalua also made sense from that angle. I just hoped I was right, for Sally's sake.

Chapter Twenty-Eight

I HAD THE CABBIE drop me a block from the hotel. It wouldn't do to drive up to the entrance and have one of them spot me before I had a plan to rescue Sally. I walked around the property when I got there and that's when I saw it. Parked in the lot at the back of the hotel was a black Honda Accord sedan with a broken right rear passenger door glass. I retreated to a diner across the street and diagonally opposite the hotel's entrance and put in a call to Lieutenant Chang.

"Criminal Investigation Division, Lieutenant Chang."

"David, I'm inside a diner across the street from the Moanalua Hotel on Kalakaua Avenue. I think I've located them."

"Yeah, Rick?"

"I found the black Accord parked in the back lot of the hotel."

"You think that's where they're holding Sally?"

"Yeah, but they know me. I can't risk running into one of them in the lobby, so I haven't been inside to talk to the desk clerk. I'm watching from here in case they leave."

"I'll be over there with Rowden right away."

"Okay, good."

I watched the hotel from inside the diner until David and Rowden arrived ten minutes after I'd called. When they walked in, I met them at the front entrance.

"Is the car still there?" David asked.

"Yes, the only entrance is there in the front of the hotel. They can't drive out without us seeing them."

"Good. I had Rowden to park the car at the back of the diner. In case they look out a window, I didn't want them to see a police vehicle parked here and get spooked. Now where's Rowden? Rowden!"

"Be right with you, Lieutenant," Rowden called. "I'm just getting something to nibble on."

"Something to nibble on," Chang said. "For the love of... That idiot. If one of those guys walks in and sees a cop, they will take off like a jackrabbit. How do you want to play it, Rick? Think I should call in patrol units to set a perimeter around the place?"

"Not yet. Let's get a room number first. As soon as Rowden finishes his nibbling, send him over to talk to the desk clerk."

"Okay. Hey, Rowden, get over here, you idiot."

Rowden joined us, holding a cup of coffee and chewing on something. "Yes, Lieutenant?"

"You have those photos we printed back at the station?"

"Yes, I've got them right here in my jacket pocket."

"Okay, go across the street to the hotel. Ask the desk clerk what room those two hoods are staying in. You might have to show the photos if they registered under an assumed name."

"Yes, Lieutenant. Can I drink this coffee first?"

"No, you blockhead. We aren't here on a coffee break. Get over there right now."

I took the cup of coffee from Rowden. "I'll hold this for you, Rowden."

Rowden left for the hotel and I sipped the coffee.

"Want to share, David?"

"No, Rick, you go ahead. Are you sure you don't want me to get you something to nibble on to go with it?"

"No thanks," I chuckled. "I'm fine with just the coffee."

After five minutes had passed, David was getting antsy. "Where is that idiot Rowden? How long does it take to ask a desk clerk a simple question?"

Five more minutes passed and then we saw Rowden strolling across the street on his way back to the diner. I finished the last of the coffee. David and I had sat down in a booth at the back beside a front window from where we could watch the hotel entrance. When Rowden walked in, he glanced around, looking lost.

"Rowden!" David called. "Over here."

Rowden beamed when he saw us and headed over.

"What took you so long?" David asked.

"I was getting the lay of the land, Lieutenant. The clerk told me Robert Lukela had rented a room this morning. Paid cash. He said he saw them leave a little later and then they came back a couple of hours ago and had an attractive blonde with them. Then they took the elevator up to their room. It's on the fourth floor."

"Did he say anything else?"

"Yeah, he said the blonde seemed unhappy. The clerk thought that was weird, but he said he doesn't stick his nose into his guests' business. Oh, and I asked, and the guy said there are forty rooms rented at the present time. He says business has been a little slow. They get little of the tourist trade on account of being an older property."

"So, you talked to the clerk, and it took you over ten minutes?"

"Well, no. After he gave me the room number, I took the elevator up to the fourth floor and walked past the room. I thought you would want to know where it was in relation to the elevator and the stairway exit."

"Rowden, did I ask you to do any of that? I told you..."

"Hold on, David. Rowden did well. That is useful information."

"Oh... okay. I suppose you're right, Rick."

My phone rang. I took it out and saw on the screen it was Sally calling. I looked at David and Rowden and put a finger to my lips, then I answered.

"Sally?"

"Rick? Oh, Rick..."

I heard a commotion and then a male voice came on the line. I recognized it. It was Lukela, the weasel.

"Well, hello, Bishop. I'm calling to let you know we have your blonde girlfriend. She's pretty hot stuff, yeah?"

"Listen, if you lay one hand on her, I'll find you and make sure you die a slow and painful death. That goes for your pal, the gorilla, too."

"Don't be like that, Bishop. As long as you do what I tell you, we won't have to hurt her."

"Okay, what do you want?"

"You remember we were talking about driving out to Halona Blowhole?"

"Yeah, I remember."

"Okay, well, since you ran away from us, you can just meet us there. Be there at eleven o'clock tonight. You show up and we'll let the girl go. Simple, right?"

"Sure, and yeah, I'll be there."

"Good boy. But don't forget this part. Don't call the police and come alone. You cross us and your girlfriend will be the one taking the dive. You got that?"

"Yeah, I got it. But I don't have a car. I'll have to take a taxi. But as soon as I get there, I'll get out and send the cabbie away. That work for you?"

"Sure, I don't see a problem with it."

"Okay, let me talk to Sally."

"Fat chance. You'll see her for a minute tonight as long as you show up and stick to our little agreement."

The line went dead.

"Was that them?" David asked.

"Yeah, it was Lukela. He made Sally call me with her cell phone, and then he took it from her. He just wanted me to know they had her. And he told me what he wanted."

"What did he say?"

"He told me to meet them at Halona Blowhole at eleven o'clock and if I showed up, they would let Sally go. And of course, he told me to come alone and to leave the cops out of it if I didn't want them to hurt Sally."

"The usual."

"Yeah."

"Okay, I think it's time to get some units out here. No way the three of us can cover all the hotel exits if they should get spooked and try to leave on foot. I'll only use plain clothes officers near the hotel and keep the uniforms out of sight."

"Sounds good."

David nodded. "I'm going out back to the car to call in and set things up."

David left me with Rowden.

"Any brilliant ideas about how we're going to get your girlfriend out of there in one piece?" Rowden asked.

"No. Why don't you put that bear trap of a mind of yours to work and come up with something? Make yourself a hero."

Rowden stroked his chin between his thumb and index finger for several moments. I hoped his brain didn't explode from thinking so hard.

"Well, we could start a fire in the lobby and then they would have to come out."

"Oh, swell, Rowden. Swell. There is nothing I'd like better than a well-done girlfriend."

"Well, I didn't mean we should burn the building down. Just a small fire would probably make enough smoke to make them come out. And I tried to think of something."

"Hey. Wait a minute."

"What is it? You think of something?"

"No, you did. Rowden, please remind me to kiss you on both cheeks later. You are on to something."

"I am?"

"Yes. The hotel has fire alarms. All we have to do is pull one. We don't need an actual fire. We only need to make those two guys believe there's a fire. And like you said, they will have to come out."

"Then what do we do after we set off the fire alarm?"

"Let me think about it for a minute. When David gets back, we'll work out all the details."

Chapter Twenty-Nine

DAVID WALKED BACK INSIDE and slid into the booth beside Rowden.

"Okay, I've set it all up. Within the next fifteen minutes, we'll have detectives covering all the hotel's exits. Patrol will have a tight perimeter set around the area in case those hoods slip by them. But, Rick. I've been worrying about something."

"I know. How do we get Sally out?"

"Yeah, if we break down the door, there might be shooting."

"Well, relax. Rowden came up with a solution."

"Rowden?" David asked in astonishment.

"Yeah."

Quickly, I outlined the plan to use the fire ruse to force Lukela and Aiulu out of the hotel into the open.

"I thought up the plan, Lieutenant," Rowden said.

"Shut up, Rowden. Shut up. I can't hear myself think over your constant yakking."

"Okay, Lieutenant," Rowden said, looking crestfallen.

"I'll pull a fire alarm," I said. "When the firefighters arrive and bust into the place, Lukela and Aiulu will think the hotel is burning down around their ears."

David nodded. "Then maybe with the distraction, they won't watch Sally too closely, huh?"

"That's the idea."

"Do you think it will work?"

"I think so. When the fire trucks show up, you can tell them what's up, and they can go into the building and make like it's on fire."

"But won't Lukela and Aiulu know it's a phony when they don't smell any smoke?"

"The firefighters can tell them the fire is blazing in the laundry in the basement, but is spreading to the rest of the building. They can tell Lukela and Aiulu they've shut down the elevators and take them down the stairwell. When they get to the ground floor, they can escort them out of the main entrance. Once they are out of the building in the open, the firefighters can shield Sally from Lukela and Aiulu, and we can take them."

"Okay. When the fire department gets here, I'll have a couple of detectives dress in firefighter gear and station them on a truck with rifles. Then if Lukela and Aiulu try to shoot their way out when we close in, the detectives can put them down in a hurry."

"Where is the room exactly, Rowden?" I asked. "You walked by it."

"Yeah, it's three doors down to the left when you get off the elevator."

"So, the front of the building?"

"Yes."

"Good," I said. "That means when those guys hear the sirens from the fire trucks, they will look out the window and see the firefighters suiting up and unrolling their hoses."

"Hey, Rick," David said. "The police always roll on a major fire for crowd control. I'll send in a couple of squad cars behind the fire trucks for some extra firepower. It will all look normal, and those hoods won't suspect a thing."

"All right," I said. "As soon as you've got your men guarding all the exits, we'll get over there and I'll pull a fire alarm."

"We better go now," David said. "We need to let the desk clerk know what's going on. And we can have him call the rooms on either side of the room Lukela and Aiulu are in. If those rooms have occupants, the desk clerk can get them out quietly in case any shooting starts before we expect it. Then, as soon as I get the word over the radio that my people are in place, you can pull the fire alarm."

Rowden drove us across to the hotel. It seemed the best option in case Lukela and Aiulu and were watching the front from their room windows. It could tip them off if they saw three guys in suits who looked like cops walking together across the street to the hotel. Rowden parked the car out of sight of the fourth-floor windows where he estimated the room was. Then we all got out and went inside.

David explained the situation to the desk clerk and told him what was about to happen. I looked around and found a fire alarm. When David gave me the thumbs up, I smashed the glass and pulled the alarm. The fire alarm klaxons sounded and strobe lights flashed all over the lobby. Only minutes passed before we heard the sirens of the approaching fire trucks.

When the trucks drove up in front of the hotel, David grabbed the battalion chief and explained the situation. The battalion chief spread the word to his men, and they unrolled their hoses and charged inside the front entrance. I supposed Lukela and Aiulu, alerted by the sirens, were watching the show from the room's windows. I got an idea and made a minor change to our plan.

I grabbed a firefighter, told him I was with the cops, and persuaded him to lend me his bunker gear. Dressed as a firefighter with a helmet and face shield, Lukela and Aiulu wouldn't recognize me. I told the battalion chief I was going up to the fourth floor with him and his boys.

"All right, Bishop," he said. "We'll take the elevator up and then my guys will shut it down. We'll spread out and start knocking on doors. You and I will go to your suspect's room and order them to evacuate."

When we got off the elevator, the battalion chief and I walked directly to the room number Rowden had given me while the other firefighters knocked on other doors up and down the corridor. The battalion chief pounded on the door.

"Yeah, what is it?" Lukela shouted from the other side of the closed door.

"Fire Department," the battalion chief shouted back. "We're evacuating the building."

"Hang on," Lukela answered. "We'll be right with you."

A moment later, I heard someone slam an interior door. Then Lukela opened the entry door.

"What's going on?" he asked. "What's with all the fire trucks?"

"There's a fire in the building," the battalion chief said. "We're evacuating the hotel."

"Fire? I don't smell any smoke."

"The fire is in the laundry in the basement next to a gas main. The whole place could go up at any minute. You've got to get out now."

"Okay, let us get our luggage and we'll take the elevator down."

I looked past Lukela into the room. Aiulu stood with his massive arms crossed in front of the closed bathroom door, but I saw no sign of Sally. I figured they had stashed her in the bathroom before Lukela opened the door.

"No time for that," the battalion chief said sternly. "Leave your luggage and get out now. We've already shut down the elevators. They aren't safe to use when there is a fire. My men will escort you down the stairwell, the designated fire exit, at the end of the corridor."

"Okay, okay," Lukela said. "Keep your shirt on." Then he turned to Aiulu. "Come on, Tiny. We have to evacuate because of a fire. We'll come back for the luggage later."

Aiulu followed Lukela out of the room. Down the corridor, a firefighter shouted, "Come on. This way." The two men sauntered down the corridor to the fire exit. The battalion chief and I followed.

I was eager to check the bathroom for Sally, but I knew making sure I kept the two hoods away from her was the best way to keep her safe. So, along with the other firefighters, I tramped down the stairs behind them. When we exited the stairway door on the ground floor, other firefighters directed Aiulu and Lukela to the front exit.

"I still don't smell any smoke," Lukela said as we all stepped over fire hoses and exited the hotel lobby to the outside.

"Hey, there are some cop cars here," Aiulu said, the first words I'd ever heard him speak. His deep voice was as ugly as he was.

"Yeah, let's separate," Lukela said. "We'll meet at the car."

David and Rowden, flanked by some uniformed officers with guns drawn, appeared from behind a fire engine.

"Okay, you two," David shouted. "That's far enough. Get your hands up and don't move."

"It's a trick," Lukela shouted, reaching inside his jacket. Aiulu's enormous right hand flashed to his waistband beneath his jacket that was as large as a circus tent.

I shouted a warning to the firefighters. "Get away from them. Get down."

"Don't try it," David shouted. But both men had their guns out, and when they leveled them at the cops, gunfire erupted.

Unarmed, I had hit the ground with the surrounding firefighters. When the shooting stopped, I raised my head and glanced around. Both Lukela and Aiulu lay face down on the driveway. Cops had pounced on them and were handcuffing their wrists behind them, but they both looked pretty dead.

"Where's Sally?" David shouted to me.

"I think they stashed her inside the bathroom in the room," I replied, stripping off the firefighter's gear. Then I turned and sprinted back inside the lobby with David and Rowden on my heels. We climbed the stairs two at a time, to the fourth floor. We burst through the open door into the room and continued through to the bathroom door. I flung it open, and that's where I found poor Sally.

Chapter Thirty

SALLY WAS ON THE bathroom floor lying on her right side in front of the bath tub, trussed like a Thanksgiving turkey. Looking at me with her widened green eyes, she was making noises, but I couldn't make out what she was saying because of the duct tape stuck over her mouth. Mascara had run down her pretty face and her long blond hair was a mess. I gently pulled the tape off her mouth and untied her. We helped her up and took her downstairs. She cried a little on my shoulder and I liked that. It made me feel so protective.

David cleaned things up a little, and the media arrived. We all piled into David's unmarked car and he dropped us off at Sally's place. An hour later, Sally had showered and changed into her silk robe. She was back to normal, and we reclined on the sofa and forgot all about Aiulu and Lukela.

"How do you feel now, baby?" I asked.

"Better."

"You want me to get Cooper to fix some dinner for you?"

"Oh, no. I'm not very hungry. You can have some if you want."

"No, no. You want to play some Canasta or something?"

"You always say Canasta is a dull two-handed game."

"Yeah, it is. How about strip poker?"

Sally chuckled. "Silly."

"Want to go to bed?"

"Ooh. That sounds a little more interesting."

"C'mere," I said, trying to kiss her.

"No."

"Come on," I said, trying again.

"No," she said, pulling away.

"What's the matter?"

"I'm mad."

"Mad? What for?"

"Because those two thugs ruined the wonderful evening I had planned."

"Want me to go?"

"Course not. But I had a big surprise planned."

"You did?"

"Yes. Believe it or not, I had two wonderful tickets for the play that opens tonight at the Diamond Head Theatre. Now it's too late to go."

"Oh, no. I'm sorry, baby. What's playing?"

"*South Pacific* and it's my favorite musical."

"Oh, no. Well, I'm sorry, baby. I'd have loved to see it with you."

"Me too."

"Well, maybe I can make it up to you," I said, getting up and sitting down at Sally's Steinway grand piano.

"Oh, Rick, that's a wonderful idea."

I played a riff on the piano. "Okay, what will it be?"

"*Some Enchanted Evening*?"

"Oh, really? Well, I'm no Giorgio Tozzi exactly, but I'll do my best."

I played the song's opening on the piano from memory, "Me-me, me-me." Then I played and sang with my own dramatic interpretation.

"Some enchanted evening. You may see a stranger. You may see a stranger across a crowded room."

"Rick!"

"I'm only trying to sound like Tozzi."

"But, honey, I'd rather you sound like Bishop."

"Oh, okay."

I continued.

"Somehow you know, you know even then. Somewhere you'll see her again and again and again."

"Oh, you're no Tozzi, but it's wonderful."

"Some enchanted evening. Someone may be laughing. You may hear her laughing across a crowded room."

"Ah, Ricky."

"Night after night, as strange as it seems. The sound of her laughter will sing in your dreams."

"Rick?"

"Who can explain it? Who can tell you why?"

"Ricky?"

"Fools give you answers. Wise men never try."

"Rick!"

"Oh, honey. What's the matter? I'm just getting to the good part."

"C'mere."

"Can't you let me finish?"

"Do you mind?" Sally said, opening the robe and giving me a glimpse of what lay beneath.

"Oh. Hm. Well, when you put it that way. I don't mind, and I'm sure Mr. Tozzi doesn't either."

Strengthened by another agreeable amorous night of repose at the home of Sally Jayne Fisher, I sallied forth the following morning feeling refreshed. I boarded the bus and rode down to my Hotel Street office.

While Lukela and Aiulu now lay in peaceful repose inside matching refrigerated drawers at the county morgue, I had left strict instructions with Cooper not to open the front door to strangers. Until I dealt with Jimmy Cho, the suspected boss of the two recently deceased Chinatown hoods, I wouldn't risk further calamity befalling my beautiful Sally.

I felt almost certain that Cho was behind the killing of Joe Wang, but I still had no clue who had murdered my client, Michelle Bai. It could have been Cho or Wang. Both had motives. Or it could have been someone else not on my radar. But finding the killer of Michelle Bai wasn't my priority. What I needed most was to determine who had murdered Joe Wang so that I could collect the one-thousand-dollar bonus from Irene Chow. That money would allow me to pay off the balance of the loan from Joe Rose and keep my promise to the intractable Mrs. Wong to pay the balance of the current month's rent. That would give me a breather of at least a month.

As I pondered my next investigative steps, I laundered some shirts in the restroom sink. Inwardly, I cursed the mistake I'd made while visiting Cho's office. I should have taken the gun from his desk drawer and given it to David Chang for a ballistics test. I'd inspected it, a 45-caliber Heckler & Koch, after Cho went beddy-bye. But I'd put it back in Cho's desk drawer. If Cho had killed Joe Wang, he had probably used that gun. After wringing out the shirts and hanging them on the clothesline, I placed a call to Lieutenant Chang. If he had Wang's autopsy report, he could tell me the caliber of the bullets recovered. If they were 45s, I'd try to break in to Cho's office and get his pistol.

Sergeant Rowden answered when I called, but I didn't hurl any of the usual insults. Rowden had given a difficult birth to the idea we had used to rescue Sally, so I intended to go easy on him for a few days. In amazement, he transferred my call to David without comment.

"Criminal Investigation Division, Lieutenant Chang."

"David, this is Rick."

"Oh, great. Okay, give it to me. I can stand it. Who's dead and where?"

"No one's dead, David. I just have a question for you."

"Well, since you didn't ruin my morning by bringing me a fresh corpse, I guess I can answer a question."

"Did you get the autopsy report on Joe Wang?"

"Yes, I did. Why?"

"What caliber bullets did the coroner recover from the body?"

"Hang on a minute, Rick." I heard David shout at Rowden.

"Rowden!"

"Yes, Lieutenant?"

"Bring me the Wang file and a glass of water for my Alka-Seltzer."

"Yes, Lieutenant."

"You sure drink a lot of that stuff, David."

"I sure do, thanks to you, Rick."

"But I haven't found you a body today. Why is your stomach upset?"

"Because you've conditioned my stomach to behave like Pavlov's dogs. As soon as I hear your voice, my stomach salivates. Only it's stomach acid, not saliva. And it turns sour."

I couldn't think of a response to that kernel of information. I overhead Rowden. "Here you go, Lieutenant." Then David. "Thanks. Now get out of here and finish those reports, mallet-head."

"Okay, I'm checking the report, Rick. Let's see. Yeah, here it is. Three 32-caliber slugs. The killer shot him from close range. The coroner found gunpowder burns on his shirt and stippling at the wound sites."

"That's disappointing."

"Why?"

"Jimmy Cho has a 45-caliber Heckler & Koch in his office desk drawer. I felt sure he killed Wang. I expected the bullets to be 45s."

"Sorry to disappoint you, Rick. But they weren't."

"Now I'm at a loss to know what to do next to find Wang's killer."

"It's unlikely Lukela or Aiulu killed him," David said. "We took large bore semi-automatics off both of them at the hotel. Besides, if Aiulu had killed him, he would have just pulled the head off Wang's torso and called it good."

"You know something, David. A 32-caliber revolver is more of a ladies' gun. I never recall taking one off a male when I was on the cops."

"Well, I've known a few cops that carried them as a backup years ago. But now everyone carries compact semi-autos. Could have been a throwaway."

"Maybe," I said. "There are no women suspects in the frame."

"Be interesting to know if Irene Chow owns a 32-caliber revolver. She's in the same business her son was and Cho still is."

"But what motive would Irene have to kill her own son? Besides, I saw her at the apartment after she discovered Joe's body. His death devastated her. I can't imagine anyone faking the grief and sadness I saw that convincingly."

"Rick, women can fool you. No one should know that better than you."

"I still don't think Irene did it. So, I guess I better go back and review everything I know. I need to know who killed Wang and soon. How about Michelle Bai? You making any progress on her murder?"

"No, but I still like your lawyer for that one."

"David, for the last time, Nicole didn't stab Michelle to death. Time to move on."

"I'm still checking her alibi."

"Hey, David."

Yeah, Rick.

"Bye."

I hung up and scratched my head a little more, searching my memory banks for clues to find a murderer.

Chapter Thirty-One

I KNOCKED OFF FOR the day at two o'clock in the afternoon, as usual. But I was so frustrated over the lack of progress on my case, I decided to spend the night at my office instead of keeping my standing dinner date with Sally. I called and asked Cooper to tell her I wouldn't be over at eight, but would see her tomorrow evening. Then I stretched out on the sofa in my office and continued trying to coax the puzzle pieces together. I'd dozed off around five, but the phone rang and disturbed my slumber. I dragged myself off the sofa and answered the phone.

"Hey, baby," the caller said.

The voice sounded familiar, but my mind was foggy from sleep and I couldn't place it right away.

"Hi," I said.

"You know who this is?"

I thought of all the girls I knew, but it was a lengthy list and I had nothing.

"I guess you forgot me already. That's disappointing. It's Lucy from the Blue Goose."

It all came rushing back to me. The cute little waif wearing the short-shorts and no bra with the slender, long brown legs and shapely bottom. Lucy Wong. No relation. When I paid the rent, I had asked Mrs. Wong. I certainly hadn't forgotten her. I had just been too busy to think about her slender, long brown legs and shapely bottom for far too long.

"Oh, sorry, angel. I was asleep and just woke up. I'm not thinking clearly yet."

"Uh-huh. This is the second time you disappointed me. You never came back to find me the other night at the club. That was also disappointing."

"Yeah, sorry about that, too. What can I do for you, honey?"

"I'm calling for Ms. Chow. She wants to meet with you."

I couldn't say that surprised me. Irene hadn't struck me as a patient person. She probably wanted a report, even though I had little to tell her about beyond my suspicions.

"Where and when?"

"Her office, silly. Here at the club. At ten o'clock tonight."

I looked at my watch. It was just past eight-thirty.

"Yeah, okay, I can make that. Tell Irene I will be there."

"Okay, handsome. I'll let her know. Maybe we can take up where we left off the other night after you finish talking with Ms. Chow."

"Hm... maybe so, angel."

"All right. See you later, baby."

"Looking forward to it."

"Kiss, kiss, baby," Lucy said. Then she hung up.

I knew Lucy was more trouble than I could handle. I'd have to sneak out of the Blue Goose again after I talked to Irene. Maybe she would let me use a rear exit.

I made coffee and thought about what I would say to Irene. Then I shaved and put on a clean shirt. I locked up and left the office at nine-thirty to walk over to the club.

When I arrived, I saw only a few cars in the parking lot and guessed it must be a slow night. As I walked across the parking lot toward the entrance, the barrel of a gun found its way between my third and fourth ribs. I guessed she must have been hiding behind the car I had just passed.

"Hello, baby," Lucy said.

"Do you really need that gun?" I asked.

"Little Lucy wants you to stay close to her," she said with a smile. "We're going to take a taxi ride."

"Wait a minute. I've got something to tell you."

"About Joe? Don't bother. I already know he's dead."

"You aren't grieving?"

"I stopped grieving for Joe a long time ago. He just used me to have a good time. That's one reason I killed him."

"You killed him?"

"Yes, with this gun."

Lucy had been smart enough to put some distance between us after shoving the gun in my side at the start. I could see it from the light cast by the club's flickering neon sign. It was a cute little nickel-plated 32-caliber revolver. I figured if I could close the distance fast, I might take it away from her, but was pretty sure she'd shoot me at least once.

"You know... I have an idea about you," I said.

"Lots of men do, baby."

"Not that sort of idea. This idea is different. My idea is you traded in Joe for a hunk of fat named Jimmy Cho."

"You're making me mad, baby. That's a mistake. I might forget what I'm supposed to do with you and kill you myself."

"Did Jimmy tell you to kill Joe?"

"Nope. I did it for Jimmy because Joe was causing him problems. But it was my idea to do it. And it made Jimmy happy when I told him. He had planned to do it himself. I just did it first."

A taxi drove into the parking lot, and Lucy waved down the driver with her empty hand.

"Come on, baby. We have a visit to make. I have more to tell you, but I'll tell you in the taxi. It's more romantic."

I walked to the taxi with Lucy behind me. With my back to the club, I didn't see the shadowy figure rising from behind a parked car in a darker area the light didn't reach.

"Don't be stupid and try to tell the cabbie anything," Lucy warned. "I'd only kill you both." She opened the back door. "Get in, baby. And sit with your palms flat on your knees."

After I got in the back, Lucy slid in beside me. She gave the cabbie an address I was familiar with. She kept the gun pressed against my ribs. Now she was too close, and I was no better off. I had no room to maneuver in the cramped backseat. If I tried to overpower her, she'd only put two or three bullets in me.

"I killed Michelle first," she whispered. "That was such a rush that it gave me the idea of killing Joe. Once you kill someone the first time, it's like a drug and you want to do it again. But I couldn't risk using a knife on Joe. He might have taken it from me. So, I got this gun from a friend."

"Why, Lucy?" I whispered, afraid to talk too loudly. I didn't want her to drill the cabbie for hearing too much. "Weren't you and Michelle friends?"

"We lived together, but weren't friends," she whispered. "She thought she was so beautiful and so important. She treated me like a child. I only played her because I learned a lot by listening to her talk. Now I'm the same with Jimmy that she was with Joe before he went to prison. I got on Jimmy's good side by being nice to him. He lets me help run the lottery and I'm making real money now. And that's only the beginning. I only keep working for Irene because Jimmy wants me there. I hear things and see things Jimmy wants to know about."

I figured Jimmy Cho would soon get a place on Lucy's hit list. Once she had fully ingratiated herself and learned all about his business, she probably wouldn't need him around anymore. It was ironic when you thought about it. Lucy worked in a profession where men used her to satisfy their ignoble desires. But she had flipped the tables and instead of getting used, she was using men. I had to applaud her ambition.

Having recognized the address Lucy had given the driver, it didn't surprise me when the cab rolled up at China Doll. Lucy got out quickly and told me to pay the cabbie. I did and then I got out. She eased me across the parking lot to the side of the building, and then back to the alley. She herded me down the alley and then up some stairs at the back of China Doll. By feel, she slipped a key into the lock of a door and unlocked it.

"Open the door, baby, and go inside."

I did and could immediately hear someone operating a printing press in another room. I'd been in newspaper offices before and recognized the sound. But what really caught my attention were the neat piles of lottery tickets stacked on a long wooden table. Thousands of them.

"Jimmy?" Lucy called out.

The press in the other room stopped and Jimmy Cho waddled through an open door, the 45-caliber semi-automatic in his fat hand.

"Well, baby, I see you've brought a friend."

"Yeah," I said. "I came to buy a few lottery tickets. You can't win if you don't enter."

Jimmy Cho chuckled. "I'm afraid I can't sell you any tickets."

"Why not? My money's good. Just like the money you take from the poor people here in Chinatown who can least afford to waste money buying lottery tickets."

"Of course, Bishop. Money is money. But if I sold you tickets, you might win the lottery. And you'd never collect your prize. Because you see, Bishop, you will not live very much longer. It just wouldn't be fair to take your money, would it?"

"How do you know I wouldn't live to collect, Jimmy? Is telling fortunes one of your side gigs?"

Cho chuckled again. "You are a little funny, Bishop. Too bad we can't keep you around to entertain us. Unfortunately, you know too much now."

"And I learn a little more every minute."

"That's why you've got to go, Bishop. That's why we have to kill you."

"You going to have your girlfriend here to kill me like the others? She bragged about it all the way here in the taxi. Seems she's developed a taste for killing."

Cho frowned. "No, I'll take care of you myself, and I'll enjoy it."

"Oh? I didn't think you had the guts to do anything yourself. You didn't show up at my office to get even. You sent Lukela and Aiulu to do the work. Then you sent them after my girlfriend and that got them killed."

"Okay, that's enough talk, Bishop. I was wrong. You're not funny. And I haven't forgotten about your blonde girlfriend. I might let Lucy pay her a visit after we've finished with you."

That got my attention. It seemed a bad idea to keep provoking him.

"Keep that gun on him, Lucy. I'll tie him up so he doesn't do something stupid."

I did nothing stupid, but I felt stupid letting Cho tie my hands behind my back. He had already told me he was going to kill me. I might as well have tried to jump him or her instead of meekly letting him bind my wrists where I could do nothing. But I couldn't resist one last repartee.

"Aren't you worried about the blood? It might get all over your nice new lottery tickets."

"Don't be stupid, Bishop. I wouldn't think of killing you here inside my club."

"So, we're taking another ride? Am I going to sleep with the fishes?"

"You'll find out, shamus."

Cho sat me down in a chair and we sat around for a while with no one speaking. I figured he was waiting for it to get later so there would be less of a chance we would run into anyone when he took me wherever he had in mind. Finally, Cho stretched, walked over and whispered something to Lucy, and then looked at me.

"Okay, Bishop. On your feet. It's time to go."

I stood up. There was nothing else to do. We all went out the door Lucy and I had come in through, and down the stairs to the alley. They herded me to a Cadillac Escalade. While Lucy kept her gun on me, Cho stooped down and tied my ankles together. Then he opened the front passenger door and helped me inside.

"Go back upstairs and finish the printing," he said to Lucy. "Leave the door unlocked. I forgot to pick up my key inside. I'll be back in a few minutes and will let myself in. You wouldn't hear me over the printing press."

Lucy nodded and then headed back to the stairs. Cho got behind the wheel. He held the gun in his left hand pointed at me and steered with his right. With my hands tied behind my back and my ankles bound, there wasn't much I could do. At speed on a freeway, I might have thrown myself at him and caused a crash. But he stuck to surface streets at a speed too slow to make that an option. No one knew where I was. And I doubted Irene Chow had told Lucy to call me, so I hadn't missed a meeting with her. It had all been a setup. I'd miss seeing Sally and Joe and David. Maybe I'd even miss seeing Rowden a little. I figured they and maybe a few others would miss seeing me, too. I knew my creditors would.

Chapter Thirty-Two

CHO MADE A RIGHT turn onto River Street. After two or three blocks, he pulled to the curb, turned off the lights, and killed the engine. I recognized where we were. Here, River Street ended and the pedestrian mall began with the statue of Chinese revolutionary leader Sun Yat-sen. The wide mall, which borders the Nuuanu Stream, is lined with shade trees, park benches, and tables where seniors gathered to play mah jongg and checkers. Plenty of takeout restaurants were nearby if you wanted to eat lunch outdoors. Sadly, they were all closed for the night. I'd been here early in the morning a few times and watched senior citizens practicing tai chi.

Cho got out and walked around the front of the vehicle to my door. He opened it. "Turn on your butt and stick your legs straight out," he ordered.

When I did that, he opened a folding knife, and standing to the side so I couldn't kick him, he cut the rope binding my ankles together. Then he told me to get out. I did so. Then Cho tossed the open knife on the passenger seat and closed the door. He eased me down River Street, back in the direction we'd come. We continued up the River Street Mall. Along the mall, extending nearly a block over to Maunakea Street, is the Chinatown Cultural Plaza. Cho herded me with his gun at my back onto the Kukui Street bridge across the Nuuanu Stream, which borders River Street. About halfway across the bridge, he stopped me.

"All right, Bishop. I think we've gone far enough."

"I know we have. But there's nothing I can do about it."

There was a gap in the masonry railing where I supposed a car had struck it. The city hadn't repaired it yet. The street department had only tied strips of wide red plastic tape across the opening with "CAUTION" printed on it and had left two orange traffic cones in front of the hole.

I could imagine why he had stopped me at the gap, but it seemed a stupid place to kill someone because we stood almost directly beneath a street lamp. There were plenty of darker spots along the bridge. In the harsh light, his semi-automatic looked as big as a cannon and I saw a sheen of sweat on Cho's forehead. He kicked the traffic cones away and then ripped down the plastic strips of tape.

"There we are, Mr. Bishop. Hmm, the stream looks inviting."

"It's probably a little cold for swimming."

"You won't mind. I've never heard of cold water bothering a corpse."

"Haven't you gone to a lot of unnecessary trouble, Jimmy? You could have done this easy enough in the alley behind China Doll."

"True. But you have too many friends among the police. I prefer to keep your body... shall we say... at arm's length. So, if I'd killed you in the alley, I would still have had to dispose of your corpse. And driving around with a dead body in the back of your car is not only messy, but risky."

"I suppose you're right."

"Now step forward into the gap in the railing with the toes of your shoes right on the edge of the bridge."

"Sure, Jimmy. Whatever you say."

I stood in the gap beneath the street lamp and looked at the lava rock walls that lined the Nuuanu Stream. The WPA had put them there in 1937 as part of a flood control project. I leaned forward and looked down at the water. I did not know the depth here. Maybe if I jumped before he shot me, I'd only break both my legs. I'd find it hard to swim with two broken legs and my wrists tied behind my back. And he might still shoot me after I hit the water before I could make it to cover beneath the bridge.

"I'll make it quick and painless, Bishop," Cho said from behind me. "I'm not a cruel man."

I figured he was still talking because he was trying to work up the courage to pull the trigger. It wasn't as easy to kill another human being as some people imagined.

"Hang on. Don't you want me to fall into the water after you shoot me?"

"I do indeed."

"Then we'd better choose another spot. There's a barge of some type down there. I'll fall right on the deck."

"What? A barge? Step back out of the way and let me see."

I backed away and to the side of the opening. I thought I caught the glimpse of a shadow flitting across the street, but wasn't sure. Maybe it was just the stress, and I was seeing things. Or desperately hoping to see something.

"You stay right where you are, Bishop."

Cho had stepped partially through the gap in the railing, but not completely. I doubted I could bum rush him and knock him off the bridge. He kept one hand anchored to the railing. I'd probably only make him mad if I tried, and he wouldn't make things so quick and painless.

After peering over the edge for a moment, Cho whirled to face me. Now that he stood almost directly beneath the street lamp, I clearly saw the scowl on his face. He looked mad enough to kill me now.

"No, Bishop. There's no barge down there. What are you trying..."

I saw the two red spots appear on his chest before I heard the booming reports of the shots. Cho looked astonished. He opened his mouth to speak, but no words came out. Then the gun fell from his hand and clattered on the pavement right before Cho fell backwards and disappeared. A moment later, I heard the splash. I suppose it was the instincts I developed while in the military. At the sound of the shots, I had dropped to my knees and then rolled onto my side. I lay there wondering if the shooter was creeping up to finish me, too. I strained my ears but heard no movement. Then I heard a car start nearby and drive away fast. After another minute passed and nothing had happened, I got back onto my knees and scooted forward to Cho's gun. I turned my back to the gun, sat down on my butt, and felt around until I grabbed the gun in my bound hands. Then I got back to my knees, stood up, and hurried awkwardly back to the Cadillac Escalade.

Back at Cho's vehicle, I dropped the gun on the grass, backed up to the passenger door, and raised up on my tiptoes. I reached for the door handle. Thankfully, Cho hadn't locked the vehicle, and the door opened. I maneuvered myself onto the passenger seat and felt around until I found his knife. After getting it positioned in my hands at the right angle, I sawed on the rope binding my wrists until it parted. I stepped out of the vehicle and closed the door. The vehicle was useless to me. The keys were in Cho's pocket and he was in the water below the bridge. I folded the knife and stuck it into my pocket. Then I picked up the pistol, stuck in my waistband at the back, and took off at a jog back toward China Doll.

Chapter Thirty-Three

I HADN'T BEEN ABLE to take Cho while he was standing on the edge of the bridge. But somebody had done in for me. The two shots had caught him right over the heart. With my wrists bound, I couldn't have grabbed him before he fell off the bridge into the stream, even if I'd been closer. From the illumination of the street lamp, I'd caught a circle of ripples where Cho had hit the water before I'd hot-footed it back to the Escalade. Then the ripples had disappeared and there had been nothing.

As I jogged back to China Doll, I suddenly realized I believed I knew who had killed Cho. There was only one person who made sense. I got back to China Doll in under ten minutes. As I raced down the alley toward the stairs to the second floor, I heard the two shots. There was no reason to hurry now. I climbed the steps and opened the back door. Lucy lay on the floor, a pool of blood spreading out from beneath her. And standing over her, still holding the gun, was the person who had killed Jimmy Cho and had just shot Lucy. I kneeled beside the body and pressed my fingers to Lucy's neck, checking for a pulse. I found none. She was dead.

"The other one... is he dead, too?"

"Yes, Ms. Chow. Jimmy Cho is dead. Both bullets struck him above the heart and he fell into the Nuuanu."

"We trusted them. Joe and I. We trusted them."

"You shouldn't have killed them."

"They killed Joe. My son..."

"The law would've punished them. Now they will punish you instead. And you've already suffered enough grief."

"I know only the law of Chinatown. Those who betray must die."

"How did you know about them, Ms. Chow? I only found out for sure this evening. That's why I haven't called you."

"I heard rumors Lucy was seeing a lot of Jimmy Cho. I became suspicious and began watching her. When she left the club tonight, I followed her, staying in the shadows. Although I thought she was waiting for Cho, you arrived. I saw her pull the gun on you, remained hidden, and overheard every word she said. Then I followed the taxi to China Doll and watched her take you inside. I listened at the door, and heard every word from Jimmy Cho, too."

"Then you followed us to River Street?"

"Yes, and waited patiently until Cho foolishly stepped into the light of the street lamp. Then I had him. I drove back here and finished it."

"I guess you didn't need a detective after all, Ms. Cho. You figured it out by yourself."

"No, Mr. Bishop. You earned your money."

Irene reached into the neck of her shirt and withdrew a wad of cash from inside her bra and handed it to me.

"Here's the other thousand. If you hadn't been at the club tonight, I'd never have overheard Lucy admitting she killed my son. She would have never confessed to me. You're not a bad detective. For a haole."

Irene flashed me a tight smile, and I chuckled at her remark.

"I don't want to. You saved my life. But I'll have to call the police. Lieutenant Chang doesn't approve of bodies lying around in back rooms or polluting our pristine water-ways."

"Yes, I know. Here, take the gun, Mr. Bishop. I have no further need of it."

"Irene, I wish..."

"I can see it in your eyes. You understand. Do you not, Mr. Bishop?"

"Yeah. I understand. That's why I wish I didn't have to call the cops."

I reclined on the sofa in Sally's living room with her curled up beside me, her head resting on my shoulder.

"Darling, you're still feeling blue, aren't you?"

"Yes, Sally, dear," I said.

"About Irene Chow?"

"Yeah... I must be getting soft, but I can't forget her face... the look in her eyes when she was talking about Joe."

"C'mere, Ricky."

Sally turned my face to hers. She kissed me long and deeply.

"There... does that help?"

"I knew I could count on you."

"I enjoy being counted on."

"Baby..."

"Uh-huh?"

"Let's go out somewhere. Some place we can dance. I'd like to dance and listen to some loud music. Very loud."

"Well, I could still get us a table at the Polynesian."

"Do you mind?"

"Of course not. You know I enjoy dancing. I'm happy for us to go out."

"Thank you."

"Rick, there's something about this case you just finished that I can't figure out."

"Can't you?"

"No. It's about that girl, Lucy. She was a flash girl, wasn't she?"

"Um.... yes, pretty flash."

"What made her give up a good-looking guy like Joe for that awful Jimmy Cho? And what made her betray and then murder her friend? That Michelle girl."

"Baby, this proves something I've always believed about you."

"What's that, Ricky?"

"You just don't understand women."

About Author

LARRY DARTER is an American writer of fiction, primarily of the mystery & detective and police procedural genres. He is best known for the nine novels written about the , wise-cracking Los Angeles private detective Malone. Darter has also written four novels based on the fictional character T. J. O'Sullivan, a female New Zealand ex-pat, working as a private investigator in Honolulu, Hawaii, three police procedural novels featuring the fictional character LAPD homicide detective Howard Drew, and five novels in a comically toned private investigator series featuring soft-boiled Honolulu PI Rick Bishop. Learn more about the author by visiting his website: https://www.larrydarter.com

www.ingramcontent.com/pod-product-compliance
Lightning Source LLC
Chambersburg PA
CBHW030232180626
46810CB00008B/3082